Ninety-Nine Problems

A Young Adult Novel
by
Gloria Dotson-Lewis

D1279731

Wahida Clark Presents Young Adult
60 Evergreen Place
Suite 904
East Orange, New Jersey 07018
973-678-9982
www.wclarkpublishing.com
www.wcpyoungadult.com

Ninety-Nine Problems
ISBN 13-digit 978-1936649426
ISBN 10-digit 193664942X
Library of Congress Catalog Number 2011917470
1. Young Adult, Contemporary, Urban Fiction, African American, – Fiction

Cover design by Nuance Art nuanceart@wclarkpublishing.com
Interior book design by Nuance Art

Printed in United States
Green & Company Printing and Publishing, LLC
www.greenandcompany.biz

Acknowledgements

I would like to thank my Father in heaven, the God of Abraham, Isaac and Jacob who has blessed me with a gift that I pray will touch the lives of young adults everywhere. I would like to thank my loving husband Marvin who always has my back and my awesome kids Deonte, Porshay and Malik for all their love and support. I would like to give a special thanks to my dear friend Linda, aka L.J. Wilson who inspired me to take my dream of working with young women to another level. This book would not be complete without you. Thanks for all you precious time and hard work. Thank you to Earl Sewell, Porshay Lloyd, Timothy Jefferson and Marquis Dotson for your great work on the book trailer.

You guys rock! I would like to thank my stress relievers Melba Simms, Lisa Sims, Diane Taylor, Monique Steward, Kimberly Scott and my sister-friend Stephanie Smith. Whenever I need to laugh, get away, talk about old times or just get something off my chest, you girls are there. Thanks to my Metra crew for your friendship and support. You make my commute to and from work every day a joy. Thank you to my mother and grandmothers who help to shape me into the woman I am today. I love you guys. Thank you to Wahida Clark Publishing for the opportunity to get my stories out there for our youth. And last but not least, thanks to the readers for picking up my book. I hope it meets your expectations.

Sincerely,
Gloria Dotson-Lewis

CHAPTER
1

I t's always a good thing to have a heads-up on other freshman, especially on the first day at Fenton Fractional High School. Crea McCloud and her best friend, Fiona Spencer had been schooled by the best and even though Crea's dad, Vincent McCloud Senior, was no longer with them, they still had their game faces on—ready to roll with whatever came their way.

Crea's nerves rocked her empty stomach like ocean waves. She realized four minutes had gone by quickly as she rushed to get to the other side of the building before the late bell rang. She hadn't slept a wink the night before in anticipation of this very moment. Seeing all the different faces and being in a new school made her feel different—nervous, yet excited.

"And some of my friends had the nerve to cry on graduation day. Humph. Not me," Crea mumbled to herself. *I'm just happy to get away from all the immature drama.*

Swiftly, she rushed past other students standing in the hall, and searched for Room 151. She seemed to be the only one worried about getting to class on time. Everyone else was playing catch-up after the long summer break. Girls ran to each other and hugged while guys gave fist pounds and one-armed hugs.

Once Crea found her room, she sat in the back of the class, one desk away from a chubby girl with micro braids who was staring into a mirror. Sensing someone was near, the girl whose pudgy face embraced deep dimples when she smiled turned to face Crea. "Hey, girl, I'm Lela. And you are . . . ."

"Crea."

"Cree?" she asked, taking out a small tube of lotion and rubbing it into her flawless brown skin.

"No, it's Cree-uh. My dad got it from the word creation," Crea said. "They teased me so bad in first grade I remember crying like a baby and asking my daddy to change my name. But once he told me why he gave me the name, I've loved it ever since and wouldn't change it for nothin'." Crea stood proudly with a slight grin on her face.

The girl tilted her head. "Hmmm . . . Crea . . . I like your name. It's pretty and different."

"Thanks." Crea smiled again. "My daddy told me he loved me just as much as God loved the world. Pretty sappy story, huh?"

"Girl, no, not at all. Actually, it's sweet. You definitely sound like a daddy's girl, though," Lela said, putting the lotion back in her purse. Crea now had her full attention.

"Yeah, I *was* a daddy's girl," she said. Crea was very close to her dad until the day he took his last breath. "He passed away."

"Oh, dang. My bad. Didn't mean to bring up sad memories," Lela said.

"It's cool. I miss him a lot, but all my memories of him are happy ones."

"Good. Girl, don't even trip. Some of us here might have dads that are still alive, but it's just the same as them being dead. Either they got ghost on their baby's mom and kid, or they're smoking the pipe or doing time on lockdown. That's just the way it is with a lot of us."

Lela flicked her hand before she spoke again. Crea blinked. "Enough of the serious talk. Anyway, we're going to be really good friends. I can already tell, girl," Lela said.

I'm not so sure about that. Crea eyed Lela's tight black T-shirt slit down the middle, exposing way too much cleavage.

Suddenly Lela turned toward the door and she drew in a breath. "Would you look at the hottie over there?" She nodded toward the boy who had entered the classroom late.

"Have a seat, Misterrrrrr . . ." the teacher shouted over the other loud voices, then waited for the late kid to fill in the blank.

"Thomas. Brandon Thomas." He looked around for a seat until someone removed their feet from a chair. He sat right next to Crea.

He is a cutie, Crea thought.

Lela winked her eye at Brandon then introduced herself and Crea. "I think I just met my future husband, girl!" Lela spoke loudly, blowing him a kiss to top it off.

3

Brandon frowned, revealing a dimple.

"Probably not. I bet he already has a girl," Crea whispered.

"We'll just see about that, won't we?" Lela responded, walking over to his desk and showing a lot of teeth and cleavage. "Heyyyy, boo," she said to Brandon, who returned a head nod. "You got a girl?"

Although embarrassed for Lela, Crea wanted to turn and face their conversation, but didn't want to seem too obvious. She pretended to search for something in her backpack while trying to ear hustle.

The sound of high heels stopped all conversation, jacking the class's attention. A tall, slender girl who looked like she'd just stepped out of the pages of *Teen Magazine* entered the classroom. All eyes turned to glance at her smooth butterscotch skin, gray eyes, and dark hair that reached the center of her back. Some of the guys whispered to each other about how fine she was while others gazed at her with their mouths wide open. The minute the girl spotted Lela's empty chair, Lela raced back to her seat.

"Uh unnn, Top Model. This seat is taken," Lela said.

Only one empty seat was left in the room and it was directly in front of Mr. Mercer. "Glamour Girl" obviously didn't want to sit there, so she glanced around the room, her eyes stopping on Brandon and remaining there for several seconds. Everyone looked puzzled as she walked in his direction.

Crea looked up at the girl when she stopped in front of her desk and pointed.

"Excuse me, but he was saving this seat for me. You're going to need to move up front, sweetie. Better for you to read

4

the board anyway." She placed a hand on her hip and eyeballed Crea.

Not on the first day, Crea thought. She wasn't a confrontational person, but she wasn't the type to let people walk all over her either. Crea stared her down, peeping the girl's three-inch open-toed shoes, the jeans that hugged her body from her ankles to her waist, and the fitted T-shirt that read: "I'm Stuck on Me."

"First of all, I don't see any names on this seat. And second, unless Mr. Mercer assigns seats, I won't be moving anywhere. Now, can you please move so I can see the board?" Crea was steaming inside, but she kept her cool.

"Degggg!" some of the students chimed, including the loudest one of all, Lela.

"What is going on here?" Mr. Mercer inquired. The class suddenly quieted down. "Here's a seat up here, young lady. May I ask your name?"

"Alyssa," she answered, walking up the aisle to the front of the class like it was a runway. She sat sideways in the empty seat, glaring at Crea and rolling her eyes. The students began talking again as if there were no teacher present. The scene in the classroom was not as Crea had pictured it.

"Can I get you guys to find a seat and tone it down in here so we can get started?" The short, stocky teacher tried to get control of his classroom, but no one listened to his pleas. A couple of guys sat on top of their desks while others shot spitballs across the room.

He turned around to face the blackboard and wrote out his name, MR. MERCER, but the students kept talking and laughing.

"BAM!"

Everyone turned in his direction with surprised expressions. The large ruler he used to hit the desk was now broken in half.

"Now that I have everyone's attention, get your behinds in a seat and shut your mouths so I can begin teaching those who don't want to end up in jail or six feet in the ground," he said in a firm, deep voice.

From that point on he had the class's undivided attention. Attendance went smoothly until he got to Crea's name. "McCloud?"

"Yes," Crea said, raising her hand.

"I know your brother, Vincent."

"Really?"

"He was in my class his freshman year, too. Showed a lot of potential, but the boy goofed off and barely passed. Smart kid, but he let his friends get him sidetracked." The teacher looked over his bifocal frames as if he could check by appearances if Vince's behavior ran in their family.

Crea could feel the new guy watching her. Brandon Thomas made her nervous for some reason. "I'm nothing like him, Mr. Mercer," she said. "Besides, I know why I'm here. To ace English."

Mr. Mercer smiled. "Good for you, Crea. Well said. Now let's get down to business. Pull out some paper and a pen. There's work to do on your first day."

Crea noticed Brandon's smirk and wondered if he thought she was a lame.

After attending three more classes, Crea met her best friend, Fiona, in the cafeteria for fifth period lunch. The line was long, but moved at a fast pace. They grabbed their food and sat at a table near the window.

"Girrrrl, did you see all the cuties around here? I almost got whiplash watchin' 'em walk the halls," Fiona said, taking a bite of her cheeseburger.

Crea shook her head. "Leave it up to you to notice all the hotties on the first day," she said, taking a small bite of her cheese pizza.

"You know me." She smirked. "So, how were your classes?" Fiona asked.

"They were all cool . . . well, almost. This chick stepped up in class frontin' and had the nerve to tell me her boyfriend, who by the way is a cutie, had saved the seat I was sitting in for her. As soon as she said that I knew there was gonna be a problem."

"You checked her, though, right?" Fiona asked, giving her a serious look.

"Of course."

"You know I got your back. I don't wanna have to start bustin' no heads on the first day of school," Fiona said. "So what's the cute guy's name?"

Crea held up one finger while taking a long gulp from her cup. "Fi, tell me why I have Vince's old English teacher, Mr. Mercer?"

"Tell me why you just switched subjects?" Fiona said, rolling her neck from left to right.

Crea blushed. "Okay! His name is Brandon. But like I said, he's already got a girl, so moving right along. Back to Mr. Mercer. You know Vince was in his class messing up, don't you? But I already told him I don't roll like that."

"He's going to be watching you like security."

"Yeah, I know. And you know how teachers never show their true colors on the first day of school? Well, Mr. Mercer don't play. He checked the entire class already."

"Never mind all that," Fiona said, turning in the direction of a guy walking past their table. "Check out ol' boy in the green Polo. Girl, he is too fine! Mm mm mm. It's like having a birthday every day up in here."

"Girl, you're crazy." Crea laughed. "This is an entirely different world than middle school, but the boys are probably all the same—just wanna smash every girl . . ."

"What? What were you gonna say?" Fiona asked, confused by Crea's sudden pause.

"Fi, look behind you." Crea pointed with excitement lighting up her eyes.

"Why? For what? Is somebody behind me?" Fiona asked, turning around.

A yellow sign with black letters taped to the wall announced cheerleading tryouts the following Wednesday.

"Oh . . . my . . . goodness!" Fiona said, eyes wide open and bursting with new energy.

"Aw, man. I can't wait!" Crea was dancing in her seat. "Fi, I'm so *geeked* about cheerleading tryouts right now."

"Me too. I'm ready to get my groove on. Maybe you can help with some of the routines too, since you were captain of our old squad back at Blackstone," Fiona suggested. "I just know we're gonna make the team."

Once the school day ended, the plan was for the girls to meet Crea's brother, Vince, in the parking lot. When Crea and Fiona arrived in the lot, Vince's car was nowhere to be found. Instead, a blue Chevy Blazer sat in its place.

They started back toward the front entrance of the school when they heard a car horn.

Fiona pointed and said, "There he is, Crea."

Crea's eyebrows furrowed and her forehead wrinkled as they walked in Vince's direction. Two guys climbed out of Vince's car and gave him a complex handshake. One guy Crea recognized as Vince's friend, Marcus. But the other guy made her freeze mid-step; her stomach clutched then violently spun like she'd been on a Tilt-A-Whirl. A small dragon was tattooed on the left side of his face. His beady, black, glassy-looking eyes stared at Crea a little too long as he walked past her. She stepped back to give him more space to pass. His angry mug and hard walk were intimidating. *He's definitely a lot older than Vince and Marcus.* Crea thought

The tattoo on his face represented the Forty-Seventh Street Dragons, a well-known gang whose turf wasn't too far from their neighborhood. As the guys walked toward the back of the school, Tattoo Face lit a blunt and passed it to Marcus. Then they disappeared behind the building.

Crea put her hands on her hips and asked Vince, "Where have you been? You get out of school at three-thirty just like us."

Vince pointed at the passenger seat. "Man, get in the car. You're my sister, not my mother!" He often said Crea sometimes forgot he was the oldest.

"I know you didn't ditch on the first day?" She waited on his response.

Vince smirked as he brushed his hair. "Crea, be easy. It's no big deal. We never do any work on the first day anyway. But you wouldn't know nothin' 'bout that, *fresh meat*."

"Whatever! All I'm saying is Mom would kick your butt if she knew you missed school. And who was that banger with the tattoo *anyway*?"

"Nunya. Man, get in the car and quit trippin' before you get left."

Fiona put her arms around Crea and Vince. "I don't feel any brotherly and sisterly love in the air. Can't we all just get along?" she asked with a wide smile.

"Shut up, Fiona!" Vince and Crea said in unison. They jerked out of her grasp and got in the car.

Vince looked over at his sister. "And anyway, Ma ain't kickin' no behind here 'cause she ain't gonna find out. Ain't that right, Crea?"

"If you wanna grow up to be a loser and disappoint Mom and Dad, then that's all on you."

Vince exhaled loudly. "Man, shut up! You ain't Ma . . . Dad either!" he said. Crea got on his nerves most days. Her nagging about him cutting class and who he hung out with was irritating him like a bad rash. She acted just like his mother instead of his baby sister. *Man, I wish Crea didn't go to Fenton. Then she wouldn't be all in my business. I can already tell she's gonna be snitchin'.*

NINETY-NINE PROBLEMS

CHAPTER 2

Principal Williams got it twisted if she expected the entire junior class to sit quietly in the auditorium and listen to her. That was next to impossible. Even *she* should have known that. First semester was quickly coming to an end, and most students were glad since winter vacation was right around the corner. The principal wanted to discuss the SAT exam with junior students interested in attending college. Many kids listened attentively, but others used the time to socialize.

Far from paying Principal Williams any mind, Vince couldn't stop laughing at Marcus's freestyle rhyme. Their homeroom class sat in the back of the ancient, dimly lit auditorium that was in need of a fresh coat of paint and some new seats. Most of the lights didn't work and the sound system was barely audible.

Vince bumped Marcus's shoulder. "Marcus, man, you need to be paying attention to Williams 'cause you could never be a rapper. Man, that sucked!" Vince's dark brown eyes squinted as he bent over laughing.

"Okay, okay, I see you got jokes, Mr. Funny Man. Let me see what you got," Marcus said, moving his shoulder-length dreadlocks out of his face.

"Check this out." Vince looked confident and said, "Yo' flow sucks like a baby on a bottle; my flow rips the runway like America's Next Top Model . . ." He popped the collar of his black T-shirt that read: "Raw."

"Whateva, man. Look at shorty ova there. Umm," Marcus said about a girl with mocha brown skin who walked past.

"That's ole girl Melinda I told you about. I hit that the other day," Marcus bragged.

"You lying."

"Shhhhhhhhhh," a light-skinned girl with a long, fire-red weave said, grimacing in their direction.

"Girl, turn around and mind ya' business!" Vince responded.

"Some of us are interested in more than just rapping or becoming dumb jocks. I need to hear, but I can't . . ." The red head's voice escalated as she rolled her eyes. "Because you two are too *stupid* to realize how important this is."

"Man, who you comin' at like that? You don't know me, shorty." Marcus stood up, his nostrils flared as he pointed in her face. "You better stop talking to me right now."

"*You* better get your finger out my face!" the girl said, standing up and knocking his finger down.

Marcus drew back his hand, but Vince stood and grabbed him just in time.

"Man, forget her. She's not even worth it." Vince tried calming him down.

14

"Yeah, you better get him 'cause he don't know me either. You think you're scaring me? I don't scare that easily," she said, rolling her neck.

Mr. Mercer headed their way and all eyes were on them. The principal told everyone to be seated, but no one heard her over the students chattering about the incident. A muscular security guard who hadn't been sitting too far away came down the aisle to assist Mr. Mercer. The guard grabbed Marcus by his extra-large white T-shirt while Mr. Mercer guided Vince toward the principal's office. As they walked down the empty hallway, Mr. Mercer suddenly stopped.

"Vince, man, what's up? You're just determined to go down the wrong path in life, huh?"

The almost six-foot tall Vince looked down at Mr. Mercer and said, "I didn't even do nothin'."

"Is that what you're going to tell a judge after you're caught with one of your boys in a gas station he just robbed? It won't matter that you didn't do anything, man. If you hang with the wrong group of people, then you'll always be associated with them."

Vince closed his eyes and shook his head in annoyance. *I'm tired of Mr. Mercer lecturing me all the time. Every time I look up, there he is looking at me.*

"I know you can't see it now, but the choices you make today will have an effect on you tomorrow. The truth is you've already got one strike against you for the color of your skin. You've gotta work twice as hard as the next man just to make it and you certainly don't want a criminal record. Vince, you know your dad would want you to make something out of yourself," Mr. Mercer said, trying to get through to him. "You've gotta do better, man . . ."

"I hear you," Vince said without really meaning it. "Leave it to you to always bring up Dad. I mean, that's cool and all." He shrugged. "But he ain't here no more, man. Ain't been here for a good minute. But I hear you. I'm all good."

"Are you? Look, man, don't use your father's death as a reason to wild out. I see what you're doing and you don't even know that you're doing it."

The thought of punching Mr. Mercer in the mouth quickly flashed through Vince's mind. Clenching his teeth, Vince said, "Dad's death ain't got nothin' to do with this, Mr. Mercer." He swept his tongue against the inside of his mouth until the anger left.

"And what about Kathy?" Mr. Mercer asked. "Don't you think you'll disappoint her if you don't live up to your potential?"

Vince wanted to say, "Man, please!" But instead he looked right through Mr. Mercer. "What about *Kathy*? She's good."

Lightly chuckling to keep his cool, Mr. Mercer said, "Man, I hope you wise up. And I know it's killing you inside that your dad's gone. I miss him a lot, too. He was like my brother. But, Vince, you've got to let go of that hurt and anger and focus on your future. If you keep going the way you're headed, you're gonna get a rude awakening, young brother. Here, take my card. My number's on there. If you need someone to talk to, just call me anytime." He adjusted his glasses and escorted Vince to the principal's office. "Take it easy," he said, gently slapping his shoulder then walking away.

16

Vince joined Marcus in the lobby area of the main office where they waited for an hour for the assembly to end. The secretary talked on the phone the whole time but immediately hung up her personal call when the principal walked in the room.

"In my office. Right now!" Principal Williams yelled as she glowered at the two boys. The principal's office was the best looking room in the building. In fact, with everything else falling apart, it looked out of place. The cherry wood executive desk and plush leather seat was fit for President Obama. The clean white walls had abstract portraits and fresh lilac tulips sat in a crystal vase on her desk.

Mad and slow-dragging his feet into her large office, Marcus said, "Where's ol' girl? She came at me first, so why she ain't in here, too?"

"Shut up, Marcus! I am so *tired* of your mess. We are still in the first semester of school and this is your third time in here. If you don't want to do anything with your life, do us all a favor and just drop out. You'll be in jail or dead in the next five years anyway. Your grades are lousy and all you do is disrupt every class you're in."

Marcus' nose flared. "She came at me like I'm a punk or somethin'. And I ain't about to let *nobody* punk me!" he shouted.

Principal Williams placed her hands on her hips and scowled. "I'm not going through this with you today. You two are on in-school suspension for a week, beginning today."

Vince frowned. "But, Mrs. Williams, I didn't do anything," he whined.

17

She ignored his plea. "You'll be helping to clean up your school from top to bottom *after* hours. I'd rather keep you both at home for a few days, but I'm sure I won't be able to get in touch with Marcus's crack head mother anyway. But Mr. McCloud, I'll be calling your mother today, and I advise you to find a new friend to hang out with. This one is bad news."

"But, Mrs. Williams . . . please . . . don't call my mother," Vincent begged.

"Well, Mr. McCloud, maybe you should choose your friends more wisely." Her eyes scanned Marcus up and down.

Swatting the air with one hand, Marcus said, "Man, whatever! I wanna know why we gettin' in-school? You can't do that."

"Really? Really? I can do anything I want, Marcus. Keep talking and I'll add a few more weeks."

"But we didn't even touch nobody!" Marcus jumped out of his seat.

"Boy, sit your butt down right now!" Mrs. Williams grabbed him by the throat with her man-sized hands. "I saw you raise your hand to slap that girl!"

Vince's eyes grew large. His heart raced with fear as he sat straight up in the chair. He'd heard rumors about Mrs. Williams hitting students to provoke them, or sometimes falsely accusing them of things they didn't do just to suspend them, but he had never witnessed it.

Marcus stood still, clenching his teeth. Both of his fists were balled tight. He could see himself being arrested and sent to juvy if he laid his hands on her. He looked Principal Williams in her eyes. "Let me go!" he said forcefully.

Principal Williams smirked as she glanced at his fists. "Go on and do it, Marcus. You're already pushing me way over the edge and you're on your way out the door for good in a minute anyway. You have no respect for your peers *or* for authority." She turned to address Vince.

"Vince, you don't want to cross me, so you better learn today that I'm not the one to be messed with." Finally letting go of Marcus's neck, she pushed him back in his seat. Marcus touched his neck and gently rubbed it. "He's going nowhere fast, but you don't have to follow—"

The phone rang, interrupting her lecture.

"Principal Williams, you have an angry parent on line one," the secretary informed her.

"Put 'em on hold, please." She hung up the phone, walked toward her door, and opened it. "Get a hall pass from my secretary and get to your classes. Meet me back here at three, and I'll have your list of duties ready. Have a good day, gentlemen." She smiled at a teacher passing by and then shut her door.

As Vince and Marcus left the office, they didn't speak a word. Marcus stormed down the hall ahead of Vince and walked straight out the front entrance. Vince went to his last class, shocked by what had just happened. The last forty minutes passed in a blur. His mind was crowded with thoughts of what his mother would say if she got a call from the principal.

Glad the day was finally over, Vince couldn't get out of the building quick enough. As he ran to his car, he saw his childhood friend, Reggie, walking to his car. "Hey, Reggie, you going to the game tonight?" Vince yelled.

"Nope, I gotta work tonight, man," Reggie replied.

"When you gon' hook me up with them new Jordans? I need some new kicks, man."

"Just come through and I'll let you use my discount."

"Cool, I'ma do that," Vince said, pulling his brush out of his back pocket and brushing his hair.

"All right, man. I'll be looking out for you. Deuces." Reggie got in his car and pulled off like he was on a mission.

Vince thought about finding a job so he could have some extra money in his pockets. The money his mother gave him wasn't enough to keep up with the latest trends. He actually admired Reggie. He kept up his grades, stayed out of trouble, and went to work every day.

Vince spotted Marcus sitting on the trunk of his car, bobbing his head to the music blasting from his iPod. Marcus was now rocking a white and black Sean John T-shirt with a matching baseball cap. When Marcus saw him coming, he jumped off the car, strolled toward him and took the earplugs out of his ears.

"What up, V? I wanna holler at you for a minute," Marcus said as they did their routine handshake.

"What's up, Money? Look at you, changing clothes like your gear got dirty."

"It did. You didn't see Williams wrinkle my shirt when she snatched me up? Man, I would've hit her dead in the eye, but I ain't goin' to the joint. Plus, I got a shorty to raise. Can't make no paper locked up," Marcus said, brushing away invisible lint from his shirt. "Anyway, V, you know Williams was lying about my moms, right? I don't want no rumors around school that I got a crack head momma, so I wanted to straighten that out with you."

Vince looked puzzled. "I figured she was lying, but even if she wasn't, I wouldn't go around telling your business like that. Everybody got a relative on drugs. My aunt Vicky on that stuff real bad," Vince said, even though it wasn't true.

"Look! My moms ain't on no drugs, so why we still having this conversation? I just don't want nobody spreading no false info."

Vince saw Marcus's mom every blue moon around the neighborhood. A blind dude could see she was on something. The fact that Marcus never wanted Vince to come by his crib was also an indicator that something was wrong.

"It's cool, Money. You need a ride to the crib?" Vince asked.

"Naw, I gotta meet this female in a minute. I'll holler at you later." Marcus put his headphones on and left.

Vince got behind the wheel, turned on the ignition, and cut up the volume on his stereo. Jay–Z's single blasted from the speakers. Vince rapped along with the song as he moved his head to the beat, glad he didn't have to be bothered with Crea and Fiona today. They had both made the Baby Dolls dance team, so they had to attend practice for the upcoming playoff game.

In no rush to get home because there was a possibility his mom would be waiting for him to walk through the door, Vince cruised around with no specific destination in mind. Principal

Williams had probably already called her. Just two weeks earlier, the school left a message about someone cutting classes. Kathy McCloud was furious and called both of her children to the kitchen to find out which one of them was guilty. Crea immediately said it wasn't her and although Vince denied it too, she knew otherwise. Her son's grades had declined after his father's death. And according to several teachers, he had become the class clown. Kathy had a long talk with Vince before the school semester began and he promised he would stay out of trouble this time, but he hadn't.

Later that same evening, as he snuck into the house, Vince overheard his mother talking on the phone.

"I don't know what I'm going to do with Junior. Mercer, I got a call today from the school saying he cut his classes." She paused. "You had to pull him out of the auditorium today? For what?" There was a long moment of silence then she continued. "That's good she has him cleaning up after school. He needs some kind of punishment. And I certainly appreciate you watching out for him. Vince Senior would appreciate it, too. Wait until Junior gets his hard-headed behind in here. Yeah, and I almost knocked his teeth out his mouth the other day for talking back. He is really getting out of hand." There was a longer pause. "I really wish he would open up and tell me what's going on, too," she said, then ended the call.

She trippin'. Ain't nothin' to open up about, Vince thought. *I'm all good.* Suddenly, she sniffed. She was crying. Guilt settled in Vince's gut as he crept back outside to avoid his mother's wrath. *Marcus should be around the block. I'll catch up with him and kill some time until she's gone to work.*

He didn't mean to cause her a lot of grief. The pain of losing his father hadn't quite gone away. If only he knew how to make the aching in his chest stop. Every time he thought of the day his dad died, he grew furious. The fact that Mr. Mercer was his dad's best friend didn't help either. Mercer rode his back almost as bad as his dad used to.

The day his father died came to Vince in a flash. Their entire family was out bowling, talking trash, and having a good time. His dad was wiping off his bowling ball when suddenly he grabbed his head with both hands and bent over in agony, falling to the floor in what seemed like slow motion. The ball dropped on the emerald carpet, just missing his foot. Vince, his mom, and Crea turned in his father's direction. Vincent Senior's eyes shut and his head hit the carpet, bouncing once before coming to a halt like the rest of his body.

Vince hadn't been the same since. His father's absence left a huge hole in Vince's heart. He missed him more than he could express. Vince wasn't ready to be without his dad. There was so much he needed to learn about life, like how to become a man. Every word Vincent Sr. spoke went in his son's ear and stayed there like the lyrics to his favorite Jay-Z song. Now who would be there for him when he needed fatherly advice?

Later that night on his way back home, Vince turned the corner of his block deep in thought. He knew if his dad were alive he would be going off on him for cutting classes, even on the first day. But Vince Jr. wanted to go off on his dad for leaving him with feelings that he couldn't make any sense of. All he knew was that he was angry at the world.

When Vince walked in the house he saw Crea sitting at the kitchen table doing homework.

"Momma left a note for us," she said without looking up from her book as she handed the paper to him. The words were written in red ink:

Had to go in to work early. Dinner is in the oven.
See you two in the morning.
Love Mom.

Vince sighed in relief, figuring he'd go upstairs and actually do some homework.

"Vince, Momma said she wants to talk to you when she gets home in the morning. I think Principal Williams called here."

His relief vanished like a flash of lightning. *Mr. Mercer always acting like he got my back, but calls mom every chance he gets to sell me out,* Vince thought.

"What did you do this time?" Crea asked.

"None of ya business!" Vince said. He ran upstairs to his room and slammed the door.

CHAPTER
3

By November, Crea and Fiona were on the grind, tackling demanding classes and homework, as well as attending cheerleading practice daily for the biggest game of the season against their rival school, Richmond South. Though their lives were pretty busy, the girls managed to talk every day about everything. But one of them had a secret 'boo' that she hadn't yet told her BFF about. Crea wanted to tell Fiona. In fact, holding it in was killing her. But she knew telling Fiona about her feelings for Brandon Thomas came with a price. Fiona would pressure her into telling Brandon or find a way to tell him herself and Crea wasn't ready for that. She and Brandon were friends and she didn't want to jeopardize their relationship if he didn't feel the same about her. Besides, he already had a girl, Alyssa.

Her cell phone vibrated, invading her thoughts.

"Hello?" she answered, scratching the black satin scarf that wrapped her sandy-brown hair.

"Hey, Crea, what time are you and Vince picking me up?" Fiona asked.

"Fi, you know my brother doesn't leave out until the last

minute. Plus, I'm ironing right now," Crea said, carefully pressing her denim miniskirt and then her pink and white

RocaWear T-shirt. "Plus, I think he's on the phone with some girl."

"Like always," Fiona said, looking toward the ceiling.

"You know the boy thinks he's a player. But whatever! Why are you so frantic about getting to school? First period doesn't start for another hour?" Crea joked. "Who you got waiting?"

"Ha ha ha. Whatever! Just call me when you're on your way." Fiona hung up.

After showering, getting dressed, and then combing her hair, Crea went to the kitchen to get something to eat.

"Crea McCloud, let's roll out," Vince shouted, grabbing his book bag from the kitchen floor.

"Wait a minute, let me grab some breakfast. And what are you hollering for? I'm right here, crazy," she said, finger combing her shoulder length hair while standing at the refrigerator door.

"Well, let's go, lil' sis. Let's go. If ya rollin' with me, we out the door, out the door," Vincent rapped.

Crea grabbed a cereal bar and took her sweet time going to her room to gather her school books. Grumbling as she went back downstairs, she smirked while listening to Vince free style his rap lyrics.

"Please stay in school because your rap game is lame," she said.

Vince smirked. "I know there's a lot of haters out here, but I didn't know I had one livin' in the same house with me."

Placing her hand on her hip, Crea said, "I'm trying to help *you out*, big brother. Leave the rapping to Lil' Weezy, please." She steepled her hands together in prayer.

Vincent pimp-walked outside with his oversized, sagging jeans showing off his black boxers. Crea followed, shaking her head. *Those pants look like they're gonna fall to his ankles at any minute.* Vince removed his brush from his back pocket and brushed the top of his fade, thinking he had to keep his waves in check.

"Get in the car, *hater*," he said, opening the driver side door of his beat up, red Pontiac Grand Am. Crea hopped in on the passenger side and he pulled off.

Four minutes later, Crea pressed a button on her cell phone, placed it to her ear, and said, "Fi, we're outside."

"Here I come," she answered then hung up.

A minute later Fiona came out of her three-flat apartment complex wearing skinny jeans, a red and white T-shirt, and black Chuck Taylor's. Her mahogany skin, slanted eyes, and high cheekbones put her in the "pretty girl" category. Her long hair was pulled back in a ponytail.

"Fiona, hurry up and get your fine butt in this car, girl. If you were a little older and weren't like a sister to me, I would have to make you one of my girls," Vince said, checking Fiona out from head to toe.

She frowned as she got in the car and sat in the back seat. "Yuck! I've known you since I was five. Wouldn't that be like incest or something?"

"It was a joke, little girl. You're still a baby, fresh meat. I mean, *freshman*," Vince said. "You too, Crea. Fresh meat!" Vince teased.

"That's okay. I might be a freshman, but you got a *fresh* cutting up this morning, *man*." Crea laughed. "Mom snapped off on you. I thought she was gonna start giving you some blows to the head." Crea kept chuckling.

"Man, whatever. Ma is always tweakin' about something. She'll be all right," Vince answered as he pulled up to the school.

"You need to quit getting in so much trouble. You're gonna give her a heart attack. You know how much she worries."

"I heard her on the phone talking to Mercer last night."

"Mercer? My English teacher Mr. Mercer?" Crea asked, suddenly feeling her stomach tossing and turning.

"Yeah. Dad's old friend from his military days."

"What do you mean 'Dad's old friend?' I don't remember him being around dad, ever," Crea said with attitude.

"He left the country when we were little. And by the time Mercer made it back here to the States, Dad was already dead. He was the best man at Mom and Dad's wedding, too. Dad's got pictures of them hanging out together in their Marine uniforms and everything."

"I haven't seen any pictures of Mr. Mercer."

Vince shrugged. "Well, Dad showed 'em to me. Mom's still got the photo album. He was a lot younger, but he pretty much looks the same. He's the shortest one in the picture." Vince laughed.

"Did he wear those thick glasses back then, too?" Crea smirked.

"Yep," Vince said, shaking his head. "And that was like twenty years ago. Ask mom."

"Nah, I don't want to get her upset thinking about Dad. I believe you. How long has Mr. Mercer been at Fenton?"

"Since the second semester of my freshman year. When Mom came to pick up my grades, she was surprised to see him. They hugged real tight. But once they went into his classroom and closed the door all I heard was her snappin'—straight up going off on him. When she came out the room her eyes were red and watery. Mercer must've apologized a million times."

Crea looked puzzled. "Why'd she go off on him?"

"Because he promised he'd visit the day before Dad died, but he never made it. And Dad was looking forward to seeing him. Shoot, he was geeked for us to meet Mercer since it had been a minute since he'd been around. We were just shorties when he first moved away. Remember the day before we went bowling? Dad said one of his best buddies was coming over. Remember?"

Crea thought for a moment, trying to recall. After a minute passed, she said, "I think I *do* remember Dad being excited to see an old friend." Crea snapped her fingers and pointed at Vince. "Yeah! He sure did call him Mercer!"

Fiona interrupted. "Does he and your mom still talk? You said she snapped out on him. I mean, is she still mad at him?"

"No, they're cool now," Vince answered.

"So do they talk on the regular? I mean, since he was so tight with Mr. McCloud and all?" Fiona asked being nosey.

29

"Naw, not really. The only reason he's been calling her a lot lately is because of me," Vince admitted.

"Oh, okay," Fiona said, writing notes down in her journal. A slight grin formed on her mouth as she glanced out the window. "What do y'all think would happen if those phone calls turned into visits, and those visits turned into dates, and Mercer and your mom started kickin' it . . . just like in that romantic comedy movie we watched, Crea? What if he fell in love with your mom? I mean, it's a real possibility. Mrs. McCloud still got it going on," Fiona said.

"Girl, naw! Get outta here with all that," Crea quickly said as she whipped her body around to face Fiona. "He's only calling her 'cause Vince keeps wildin' out." Then Crea added, "He better *not* be trying to push up on my mom on the DL. Moms only got one husband and he's dead."

"What do you guys want her to do? Be single forever? I wish my mom would try to date, but she works too long and hard. As long as the man is respectful, has a decent job, and treats her well, then I think it would be cool to have a step dad around the crib," Fiona said.

Crea rolled her eyes and slightly pursed her lips. Fiona was truly getting on her nerves about her mom dating any dude, let alone Mr. Mercer.

"Maaaaan, Mercer's always preaching to me like he's Dad. *Go to class. Stop hanging around with those clowns before you end up in jail,*" Vince mocked. "Mom was tellin' him all my business about what I'm doin' at home and at school. He's always talkin' about what I need to do—be responsible—blah, blah, blah. What he needs to do is get him some business. He didn't even show up when it counted anyway. Where was his *responsibility* to Dad as his best friend?"

"True," Crea said. "No sense in him calling Mom now. I don't have any trouble in his class and that was two years ago when you were his student. So he should've come around when it counted."

"Anyway," Vince said, changing the subject, "Do y'all need a ride home?"

"No, we have practice before the game tonight. And I hope that cutie pie stops by the gym again," Fiona said, checking her lip gloss in her compact mirror.

"Who? That thuggish-looking guy you pointed out the other day? I bet he ain't no good," Crea commented.

"I just said he was cute. It's not like I'm trying to marry him or nothing. I don't even know his name and he didn't try to holler at me anyway. He just kept staring me down."

"Fiona, get your hot butt out of my car and go to class," Vince said, looking at her through his rearview mirror.

"Just make sure *you go* to all of your classes today while you're worrying about me. You're the one about to get a beat down by your moms." She jerked like she was going to punch Vince, and then fell out laughing.

Unfazed, Vince released a loud sigh. "Whatever, man. You just make sure you keep your eyes off thug-life before I have to tell ya moms," Vince shot back. "You're the one that's gonna get a beat down."

Crea didn't get out the car, but told Fiona to go ahead. Once Fiona was out of earshot, Crea turned to Vince and said, "I don't want Mr. Mercer calling Mom. That's not cool at all and

I'm gonna make sure I tell him that. Where has he been the past two years since Daddy's been dead?"

Vince shrugged. "I don't know, ask him. Maybe he felt guilty about the situation. You know, for not visiting Dad before he died. Maybe that's why he stayed away. Who knows?"

"Well, whatever! You need to stop giving him reasons to call our house. I don't know what's up with you, but get it together, player."

"Do you, Crea," Vince stated. "I'm chillin'."

"Oh, don't worry, I will." Crea got out the car and slammed the door.

CHAPTER
4

Principal Williams was no joke. She wasn't lying about making Vince and Marcus clean the school from top to bottom. They wiped down lockers, dusted school trophies, and cleaned windows and blackboards. They were relieved today was the last day of the suspension. It was going on five o'clock when they finally finished their long list of to-dos, which had twice as many tasks as the previous days.

Vince dropped Marcus off at the corner store two blocks away, then went to get something to eat before going to play ball at the park. It was warm outside, so he already had his windows down. The weather was the one thing he loved about living in the "Dirty South." It never got extremely cold.

Today reminded Vince of the long rides he and his father used to take up to the lake to go fishing. They would let all the windows down and enjoy the warm summer breeze. He enjoyed their family vacations, but the outings with him and his dad were the ones he treasured most. He recalled one fishing trip they took when he was about twelve.

"Dad, remember when you said I could talk to you about anything?"

"Of course, and I meant that, son. You got something on your mind?" Mr. McCloud curiously looked over at Vince.

"Last night I had a dream I was fooling around with this girl from my class. And when I woke up this morning, my boxers were wet."

His father chuckled. "Son, have you ever heard of a wet dream?"

"Yeah, I think so."

"Well, that's what you experienced. It's normal. All boys have them around your age. Your body is changing and you're thinking about girls in another way now. We'll definitely need to start talking more about sex."

"You remember when you first had one?"

"Oh yeah. I remember it like yesterday." Vince's dad smiled at the memory. "I woke up with a huge smile on my face. When I got up and sat back down on my bed, my butt was wet. I thought I had wet the bed, so I pulled the sheets off and went to the basement to put them in the washing machine before my folks woke up. After that, I jumped in the shower and put on some fresh clothes. When my dad got up, he asked me why I was washing so early in the morning. I started to lie, but I just went on and told him the truth. My father laughed so hard he almost fell off the edge of my bed. I sat there so humiliated. He finally told me that I didn't wet myself; I'd had a wet dream. When he explained what it was, I felt relieved."

Vince Jr. giggled at his father's story. "Dad, I did the same exact thing. Mom asked me why I was washing so early, but I told her I spilled something on the bed."

They both broke out in laughter.

The honking horn behind him interrupted Vince's thoughts. He drove up to the drive-thru intercom and placed his order. Vince sighed, but suddenly turned his attention to the girls sitting at the outside table laughing.

One girl with light-brown skin had a forehead like Tyra Banks. A little ponytail stuck out of a rubber band in the back of her head. Her friend was a little lighter with a stylish short hair cut. Vince kept his eye on her much longer. He liked what he saw and decided to go talk to her after getting his food. The car behind him honked at him again.

"Okay, okay, be easy," Vince said, seeing that the two cars in front of him were now gone. *I've gotta talk to ol' girl with the short hair cut*, he thought. "She's fine," he said out loud.

Vince picked up his food and checked his bag to make sure the order was correct. He parked so he could keep an eye on the dime piece while he ate. Once finished, he pulled down his visor mirror, brushed his hair, and smoothed out his eyebrows before opening his door. With an attractive smile and a lot of confidence, he approached them and sat down beside the one with the short hair.

The girl tilted her head and raised one eyebrow. "Who are you and who said you can sit here?" she asked.

"Oh, I'm sorry, shorty. My name is Vince. I saw you sitting over here looking all good, so I thought I'd come holler at you. What's your name?"

She smirked. "It's Tameka, but I still didn't say you could sit at our table."

His dimples deepened as he smiled. "You're right." Vince stood. "Is it okay if I sit here next to you?"

She looked him up and down, letting her grin show her approval. "I guess so, since you asked so nicely."

Little Ponytail smiled and softly kicked Tameka under the table when Vince asked if they wanted a ride home. As they walked to the car, they looked at each other and grinned.

"You're not some kind of serial killer or rapist are you?" Tameka's friend asked as she got in the back seat.

"Naw, shorty, I don't get down like that," Vince said. But what he really wanted to say was: "If I was, you wouldn't have to worry. I wouldn't touch you with somebody else's hands."

"Good, I don't wanna have to cut nobody." She and Tameka laughed.

As Vince pulled out of the parking lot, Tameka told him to head south. They only lived four blocks away from McDonald's. Vince was surprised he had never seen them before. In fact, his boy Tray lived on the next block where he'd hung out many times in the past. He'd have to ask around about Tameka. Before he could ask her what school she went to and if she knew some of the same people he knew, she was directing him to pull up in front of a beige ranch-style house with rickety-looking stairs.

Once he parked, Little Ponytail thanked Vince for the ride as she exited his car and waited for Tameka on the porch.

Vince turned to face Tameka. "So, since I was nice enough to give you a ride, can I get your number?"

Tameka blushed. "I guess I can do that. Give me your cell phone and I'll put it in for you."

Vince handed her his out-dated phone. Tameka entered her number, got out the car and walked to her porch. He glanced at her pretty, smooth legs and big behind. *I'll have her in my bed in no time. Bet she's a beast too.* With his mother at work and Crea doing extra-curricular activities after school, it wouldn't be hard to arrange. He had done it many times before without any problems. Out of nowhere his father's voice popped in his head. *"Remember son, what looks good to you is not always good for you."* The voice sounded so clear. Vince had to shake it off.

I'm trippin' for real. "I'll give you a call later, shorty."

"You do that. Thanks for the ride, Vince," she said, waving good-bye.

Vince turned up the volume on his radio as he pulled off. Jay-Z was rapping about 99 problems. "Glad I ain't got none," he said as if Jay-Z could hear him. He smiled, thinking about Tameka. "Yeah boy, I'm getting ready to add her to my list. I just hope she falls in the VIP section."

He headed for the park where there was always a basketball game being played. He was sure to see some of his boys shooting hoops and talking trash. He found a parking spot at the end of the block, got out the car and pulled his sagging jeans up over his waist. He brushed his hair as he walked over to the court in search of familiar faces.

"What up, Vince?" a tall, stocky guy with dark skin hollered.

"What up, Crazy Mike?"

Mike was the other guy Crea saw getting out of Vince's car on the first day of school. Crazy Mike was a well-known drug dealer around the neighborhood, who didn't hesitate to shove a gun down your throat if his money came up short. One day Vince saw Crazy Mike pistol whipping one of his workers in broad daylight in front of the liquor store. The guy was begging Mike to give him a chance to get the money, but Mike wasn't trying to hear it. He pulled out his nine-millimeter and smashed him on the head with the butt of the gun. Blood squirted everywhere and the boy fell to the ground. Mike kicked him in the back, then turned and walked off with two other guys following behind. They were all laughing and giving each other high fives. Vince later found out the guy Crazy Mike pistol whipped was Mike's own cousin.

"Yo, V. Did you think about our conversation from the other day? There's lots of money to be made out here. I'll teach you the hustle and I *guarantee* you'll make at least a G a week. You look like you can use a new pair of shoes, son. Those played out last week. These the latest kicks out now." He pointed to his spotless Gucci gym shoes.

Not the least bit interested, Vince looked toward the basketball court. "Mike, man, I told you I appreciate the offer, but I'm straight." The money sounded good to him, but he had seen and heard what Mike did to workers that messed up his money and he didn't want any parts of it. Mike was cool as long as you didn't work for him.

"If you change your mind, you know how to get at me." Mike turned and jogged across the street to his pearl-white

Cadillac Escalade. Vince thought of owning a car like Mike's, but he wasn't nearly ready to do what it took to get it so soon.

Vince sat on the bleachers and watched as the players did all kinds of stunts that would never be allowed in professional ball. Street ball was more entertaining. Many of the guys had serious skills and talent, but would never make it to the NBA. They would only be stars in the 'hood.

Bending down to tie his shoes, Vince suddenly heard screeching tires and gun shots ring out. He didn't try to figure out where they were coming from. He just ran in the opposite direction like everyone else. Holding up his jeans to keep them from dropping, he jumped over a girl who had fallen on the ground right in his path. When he reached the baseball dugout, he sat on the ground, held his head back against the wall, and took a few deep breaths. Gunfire in his neighborhood was nothing new, but it still shook him up every time.

"Man, come on, the coast is clear," a skinny kid with braids said to Vince.

Vince walked back toward the basketball court, seeing a group of people crowding around the playground area. As he moved closer, he saw a young girl on her knees in the middle of the sandbox screaming hysterically. She held a toddler in her arms whose lifeless body and clothes were soaked with blood. A couple of guys came over and one of them tried performing CPR on the child, but the child didn't respond. This was the third person to die in his neighborhood in the last two months. All he could do was shake his head and go home to his safe haven. He knew without a doubt that 'the game' wasn't for him.

NINETY-NINE PROBLEMS

CHAPTER
5

A big time attitude sat on top of Crea's shoulders. Mr. Mercer could tell something was wrong with her as soon as she stormed her way into his classroom. Anger set in Crea's tight jaw line as she flopped down in her seat, mean mugging Mr. Mercer. She crossed her arms and exhaled loudly. Puzzled by her actions, he turned to write the classroom assignment on the board, making a mental note to speak to Crea when class was over.

Alyssa walked in the room three minutes after the bell rung. Being late for class was nothing new for her. Crea believed she did it just for the attention. Alyssa walked up to Brandon, standing with her back to Crea.

"Why didn't you wait for me by the locker?" She pouted and crossed her arms in front of her chest.

"I wasn't about to be late and have Mr. Mercer trippin' on me," Brandon spoke in a soft tone.

"I'm late all the time. I ain't thinkin' about him." She smacked her lips.

"That's your problem. You have no respect for others," Crea said. "Like right now you're standing here with your butt in my face. If you don't move, I'm gonna have to make you."

Alyssa turned around to face Crea. "I know you're not talking to me, sweetie!"

"Humph. You're the only one standing here, *sweetie*. Brandon, you better get ya girl before I hurt her," Crea said without taking her eyes off Alyssa.

"Don't let these high heels and good looks fool you. You don't want none of this," Alyssa said.

Crea stood to her feet just as Mr. Mercer turned to face the commotion.

"What's going on? Alyssa, why are you over there when your seat is up here?" Mr. Mercer pointed to the seat in front of him.

Alyssa turned toward Mr. Mercer. "I had to return something to Brandon."

Mr. Mercer looked over his glasses as he addressed her. "Every day you walk in late, disrupting the class, and I've asked you several times to get here on time. You need to go the principal's office, now." Mr. Mercer held out a hall pass.

Alyssa reared her head back and frowned. "For what? I'm not going to the principal's office. I was only a minute late. You're making a big deal out of one minute?" Alyssa sat down in her seat, ignoring Mr. Mercer's extended hand.

"You need to get up, take this hall pass, and go to the main office now," Mr. Mercer demanded. "I've talked to you on several occasions, Alyssa. If you can't follow the rules like everyone else, then you don't need to be here."

42

"She needs to learn some respect!" Crea stated.

"You better shut up talking to me before I—"

"Crea, I can handle this," Mr. Mercer interrupted. "Class, I want you all to be quiet and stay seated until I return. Let's go, Alyssa." He nodded toward the door.

"This is so stupid!" Alyssa mumbled as she got up and walked out the door.

Brandon shook his head and turned to face Crea. "Anyway. What's up, Crea? Who are you mad at?" he asked.

"Nobody," she quickly answered, ignoring him by staring ahead. "Ya girl just irks me sometimes."

"You were mad before she even came in the door. What's up?"

"I said *nothing*," Crea answered.

"Girl, stop frontin'. You mad at somebody. You got wrinkles in your forehead," Lela said, crashing in on the conversation.

"I don't want to talk about it," Crea said with a frown.

"Well, excuuuuse me, funny actin'!" Lela replied before facing forward.

Mr. Mercer walked back in. "Open your books to page one thirty-six," he told the class. After checking to make sure the entire class followed his instruction, his eyes once again settled on Crea. She sat in the same stubborn position with her book closed.

"Miss McCloud, are you okay?" he asked.

"Yup. I'm cool."

Mr. Mercer thought she sounded just like her brother, Vince. He raised his glasses and stared at Crea for a brief moment. "Class, read CHAPTER ten, and then answer the CHAPTER questions at the end."

"Crea, open your book, girl," Brandon whispered. "What's up? What are you trippin' on?"

"I said I'm good, Brandon."

Mr. Mercer was amazed at Crea's behavior. His mouth turned down just a bit and his eyebrows lifted in curiosity.

"Crea, I'd like to see you in the hall, please."

Crea stood. "Let's go," she said. "I'd like to see you, too." The class ooh'd and ahh'd behind her comments. She stormed straight ahead as Mr. Mercer followed and closed the door behind him. Crea wasted no time getting to the point.

"Mr. Mercer, what's going on? Are you trying to hit on my mom by using Vince as an excuse to keep calling the house? I mean, why are you calling her so much all of a sudden? 'Cause I hope you're not trying to push up on her. It hasn't even been that long and you're not supposed to do that to your friend."

Mr. Mercer smiled. "Ah-ha. So you thought . . . oh, man. Crea, your mom is like a sister to me. And I loved your father like a brother. Your dad saved my life when we were in the military. I'd never disrespect him that way. Already, I feel like I let him down by not coming to see him before he passed away. I should have come when he asked. I was so busy getting settled in. I didn't know that he would . . ." He swallowed to keep from getting choked up and quickly turned away.

Dang, I don't want the man to start crying, Crea thought. "Say, I didn't mean—"

Mr. Mercer turned to face Crea. "Listen, I just want you guys to be successful, just like your father would want. Vince

44

Jr. is lost right now, okay? He's raging and acting out, crying for attention, but he won't let anyone in. I know he misses his father a lot. I just worry about him because the deck is already stacked high against him. If he doesn't get it together soon, he'll be dead or in jail. But you, I think you'll be all right, *Crea*, named for God's creation." Mr. Mercer smiled.

Crea couldn't even keep a straight face and grinned proudly. *He definitely knew my father*, she thought.

"Are we cool now?" Mr. Mercer held his hand out for a pound. "No crushes on my end, but I think Mister Brandon Thomas may have one on you. You guys seem to be close buddies." He smiled.

Crea could not hide her smile as she softly pounded her small fist against her teacher's larger one. "Naw, Mr. Mercer, it's not even like that. He's got a girl. We're just friends."

"If you say so, Crea," Mr. Mercer said. "Let's go back inside."

"Mr. Mercer, where have you been since Dad passed away? Why haven't you come around? I know you didn't start calling until recently because I always answer the phone. I live on it."

Mr. Mercer half-smiled. "I took a leave of absence to deal with some things I hadn't reconciled with your father's passing, but I know in my heart he forgave me and I'm able to be a better teacher and man. And this is getting pretty personal and I'm feeling a bit uncomfortable. So, can we have a productive day in my class now?"

"Definitely." Crea smiled and went back inside.

NINETY-NINE PROBLEMS

Crea couldn't wait to get out on the gym floor. She and Fiona were getting dressed in their red and white dance uniforms for the basketball game. They had been practicing two hours a day, six days a week, for the last month and were excited that this night had finally arrived. Crea was nervous, but Fiona, on the other hand, loved being the center of attention. She looked older than her fifteen years; grown men often approached her on the street. Her 38C bra size, thick thighs, and hefty behind always fooled them into thinking she was at least eighteen years old. But for those who really cared, her conversation let them know otherwise.

The twelve-girl group lined up outside the gym before the music blared from the speakers. The Baby Dolls cheer-dance team took the center of the floor. Twelve bodies moved in unison to perform a couple of cheers, and finally a tall pyramid. But once the hip hop beat started, the entire gymnasium could feel their confidence growing as they smoothly glided across the floor and performed tough stunts that wowed the audience. The routine ended, and the crowd stood to their feet, clapping and hollering in approval.

Crea noticed her friend Brandon in the bleachers and waved frantically to get his attention. Alyssa elbowed him when Brandon returned her wave. Alyssa glared at Crea.

What is wrong with that jealous, crazy girl now? Crea shrugged and continued on to the locker room. She and Brandon had become fast friends, but truth be told, Crea was very attracted to him and thought about him all the time. He was so easy to talk to and he kept her laughing, but she kept her feelings to herself. Although Fiona suspected she liked

46

Brandon, and even accused her of talking about him all the time, Crea never admitted it.

Crea and Fiona ran to the locker room arm-in-arm screaming in excitement along with the other girls. They knew their routine was flawless from the reaction of the crowd. They got dressed in their street clothes and headed back to the gym to watch the remainder of the game.

When the fourth quarter ended, they walked around in search of Vince. "I was so nervous at first," Crea said to Fiona. "But once the crowd started moving with us, I was fine."

"Girl, we were hot out there," Fiona said as she pulled her hair into a ponytail.

"Yeah, y'all did y'all thing. What's your name, cutie?"

Fiona looked up. A guy sporting an uneven afro stood in the bleachers looking down at her. He was the color of a paper bag, with dark eyes and a wide nose. As he approached her, the dragon tattoo on his left arm caught Fiona's eye.

"Fiona. Who's asking?" she flirted back.

"Romero, but my friends call me Romeo."

Crea rolled her eyes. *Look at this broke-down American Gangster trying to holler at Fiona.* Instantly, there was something she didn't like about the guy. She couldn't quite put her finger on it, but he seemed like the type her father warned her about.

"Fiona, there's Vince. We better catch him before he leaves," Crea said, looking the tattoo bandit up and down.

"Go catch him, I'll be right there." She turned to Crea and mouthed the word "go," so she could get a few more minutes alone.

"I can wait. You won't be here long anyway." She glared at him. "He's not even worth wasting your breath, if you ask me," she mumbled.

Fiona tilted her head toward the door with a quick snap, giving Crea the hint to beat it. Crea rolled her eyes and walked toward Vince's car.

"Your friend doesn't like me much, does she?" Romero asked once Crea was out of ear shot.

"Why would you say that? She doesn't even know you," Fiona said.

He shrugged. "It don't matter," he said. "You a dime." Romero licked his thick lips. "You the one I'm tryna get with anyway."

Fiona smirked. "Really? And how do you suppose you'll make that happen?"

"You'll just have to wait and see, but in the meantime, can I get your number or something?" He took his cell phone out of his back pocket and handed it to her. Fiona entered her number in his phone. He looked her over in awe of her big breasts that could hardly be contained in her fitted T-shirt.

"Well, I gotta get out of here. Call me sometimes," Fiona said. She smiled and switched toward the exit.

"Oh, you'll definitely be hearing from me, sexy," he said, nodding his head.

Fiona wore a huge smile as she approached Vince's car. Crea didn't know what Fiona saw in that Romero guy. *He isn't even cute, and I hope this doesn't get serious.*

"Girl, dude has it going on. Did you see his guns? He's gotta be doing some serious workouts at the gym. I wonder if he'll call me tonight . . ." She stopped in mid-sentence when her cell phone vibrated. Unzipping her small imitation Coach purse, Fiona pulled out her phone, but didn't recognize the number. She answered anyway.

"Hello."

"Hey, sexy, I was just making sure you didn't put a bogus number in my phone. And now that you have my number on your caller-ID, lock it in so the next time I call you'll know it's me."

"I'll do that." She giggled and hung up the phone.

"Who was that?" Crea questioned.

"Girl, that was him! He said he was making sure I didn't give him the wrong number. I've never known a guy to do that before. He must be really feelin' ya girl." Fiona walked with an extra switch in her hips.

"Whatever!" Crea laughed. "Does he go to our school?"

"I didn't get that far because I was being rushed, remember?"

"Who y'all talkin' about?" Vince asked, butting into their conversation when he walked up and unlocked the car.

"Some dude named Romero or should I say *Romeo* as his *friends* call him," Crea said sharply.

"Romeo? Nope, you don't even wanna mess with dude, Fi. He's not your type."

"My type? What do you know about my type? It sounds like you're being a hater to me."

"Yeah, whatever. But don't say I didn't try to warn you."

"Warn me? This coming from the boy who tries to smash as many girls as he can. And don't you have some other business you gotta handle, like cleaning up the school for being disruptive during an assembly?"

"Ooooh, you got jokes. That's all right. I'm still a player, though. And since you're like my little sister, I'ma keep it one hundred. Romero ain't no joke. You need to get at some other dude."

"Thanks for the advice, *hater*," Fiona said. "That's what I'm going to tell all your little girlfriends—'get at another dude.'"

"Don't say I didn't warn you when your little feelings get hurt."

"Like I said, thanks for the advice, hater!" Fiona said.

CHAPTER
6

Fiona talked about Romero so much Crea could barely stand to listen and today was no different than any other. As soon as they sat down at their lunch table she started "Romero-ing" her to death.

"Girl, look at the necklace Romero bought me," Fiona said, lifting the thin gold chain with the heart-shaped charm from her chest so Crea could get a better look.

"Yeah, cute." Crea gave the best fake smile she could manage. But what she really wanted to do was scream to the top of her lungs, *"Shut up!"*

"He said that as long as I have this around my neck, I'll always have his heart. Is he sweet or what?" Fiona's smile was as big as the walking Kool-Aid pitcher on the commercial. "He's supposed to take me out to eat after school. You wanna hang out with us?"

"Huh? Uhhh, no. I have too much homework," Crea quickly said.

"You sure? Romero's treating."

"I'm sure." Crea turned her head and rolled her eyes. She felt like gagging at the very thought.

"So, what's been up with Ms. 'I'm Stuck on Me, Alyssa?'" Fiona pulled her lip gloss out of her purse, brushed a fresh coat over her thin lips, and smashed them together.

Crea was relieved when Fiona changed the subject. "Ms. 'I'm Stuck on Me' got transferred out of the class. She was causing problems every other day, so I guess Mr. Mercer just got fed up."

"Really? Well, now you can have Brandon all to yourself." Fiona raised her hand for a high five. Crea left her hanging.

"Whatever. Just because she's no longer in the class doesn't mean she's no longer in the picture. Brandon will probably work my nerves even more talking about her." Crea still hadn't admitted out loud that she had feelings for him. She remembered the first time Brandon walked into their English class late and sat down next to her. *Oooh, he was so fine.* Crea laughed at herself. Brandon was only a couple of inches taller than her, maybe about five-feet seven-inches with a neatly low-cut fade and an attractive smile. Instead of introducing herself first and being flirty, she remembered what her father had said: "The male is always supposed to pursue the female." She was glad Brandon had introduced himself first.

Her classmate, Lela, wasted no time getting all up in Brandon's face until he flat out told her that he had a girlfriend. She was already sitting next to a guy who she claimed to like, but he wasn't interested in her. Lela thought he was playing hard to get until he finally had to tell her to back off. Seeing

Lela in action made Crea crack up. Guys didn't like loud girls who felt all eyes had to be on them. At least that's what she thought until Alyssa came through the door. Right away Crea thought she was an airhead, but that didn't stop the guys from drooling over her.

About four years back, some girl had written her brother, Vince, a letter and gave it to Crea to give to him. Crea took it straight to her dad instead. He sat at the kitchen table reading the newspaper.

"Hey, Daddy, guess what?"

"What is it, Princess Crea?" Vincent Senior turned the page and read the next headline.

"Tamara from next door wrote Vince a letter and asked me to give it to him." She held the folded sheet of paper in her hand.

"She did?" he asked, lifting his eyes from the printed words to give his daughter his full attention.

"Yeah. Wanna see it? It says, 'Will you go with me? Yes or no?'" She began to giggle at the words.

Her father closed his paper and lay it down. "You opened his letter? Crea, it's not right to go through other people's things. You wouldn't want Vince in your room snooping through your things, right?"

"No, Daddy," Crea answered in a lowered tone while looking down at the floor.

"Well, don't let it happen again. Are we clear?"

"Yes, Daddy."

NINETY-NINE PROBLEMS

Vincent Senior exhaled, looking thoughtfully at his daughter. "Since you did read it, let me tell you something, Princess. Girls are not supposed to ask boys to *go* with them. The boy is supposed to ask the girl. So when you get old enough to date, you'll know that he likes you when he comes to you. Boys think girls are easy when they chase after them and boys don't like easy girls. But they'll surely use them up and then tell all their friends about it."

Crea never forgot her father's words. And since Brandon introduced himself and eventually started treating her more like a sister, she figured she wasn't his type anyway. But they became really close friends. Crea looked forward to her English class she had with Brandon, and sometimes found herself rushing to class, even though she was in no hurry to hear about his little girlfriend, Alyssa.

Crea thought Brandon was a nice guy. He was smart and didn't do dumb things just to fit in like most of the other guys in her class. He talked to her about everything, especially Alyssa. Crea thought Brandon could do better, but she never once told him that. She couldn't be sure if the reason she didn't think Alyssa was good enough for Brandon was because she wanted him for herself, so she kept her opinion hidden. If he needed someone to talk to, she would just be there.

Alyssa was pretty and didn't hesitate to flaunt it. Crea just couldn't figure out why she felt so insecure when it came to Brandon, always wanting to tag along with him and his friends when they hung out. Whenever he tried to tell her no, she'd start an argument and tell him it was over. After the argument, Brandon would cancel his plans and hang out with her at the mall or the movies. It seemed like they argued at least three times a week.

As Crea sat at her desk listening to Mr. Mercer, she felt someone tapping her on the arm. "So, are you going to the all-white freshman dance next month?" Brandon whispered.

"Yeah, I plan on going. It sounds like it'll be fun."

"I don't really care one way or the other, but Alyssa is making a big deal about it," Brandon said.

"Are you love-birds going to dress alike?" Crea laughed, teasing Brandon.

"You are so corny. You going solo or with one of your girls?" he asked.

"Why do I have to go by myself or with one of my girls? I can't have a date or something?" She frowned.

"Crea, stop frontin'. You know your mother don't play that."

"I'll have to remember to stop telling you all my business. Besides, what my mother doesn't know won't hurt her."

"Well, I gotta check this dude out before you make any final decisions," Brandon said.

"Boy, please!" Crea waved him off.

"I would actually rather kick it at the party with my boy, Sean, but you know my girl is not having that. She be on me tighter than the elastic on my boxers. It's cool most of the time, but sometimes I just need a break. You feel what I'm saying?"

"Yeah, I hear you, but have you talked to Alyssa about it? We've discussed this before.. Just talk to the girl and tell her how you feel. Maybe then she'll give you some space. Or do you think she can read your mind?" she asked, giving him a goofy smirk.

"You know how sensitive she be acting. She'll probably start crying or something. So if it's that simple, tell me how should I say it?"

"Just tell her you miss hanging with the boys sometimes and you want to hang out with them every once in awhile without her getting upset. My dad always used to say 'honesty is the best policy'." Crea picked dirt from under her fingernail.

"I'm going to take your advice and it better work," Brandon replied.

"Either you take it to her, or you deal with it over and over again. You have to make the decision. But if you don't talk to her about it, I don't want to hear about it anymore. Understood?" Without a hint of a smirk, Crea looked Brandon right in his dark brown eyes. Although she was glad that Brandon felt he could trust her with his relationship drama, Crea was truly getting sick of the subject. Alyssa needed to grow up, but Crea knew it wasn't her place to say it.

"I hear you, I hear you," he replied with a smile. The bell rang, ending their English class. He hugged Crea as they walked out the door.

"Thanks, Cee. What would I do without ya?"

"Probably worry somebody else to death." She playfully smiled, elbowing him. Crea wondered if Alyssa was going to have a diva attack once Brandon told her he wanted to chill out with his homies.

CHAPTER
7

It was on and popping. Vince picked up Tameka (his McDonald's hook-up) from her school and brought her back to his house. Only a week had passed since they'd met, and he had already talked her into coming back to his crib. He figured he'd hit the skins within the next twenty minutes. His mother was at work and Crea would be at cheerleading practice for another hour and a half. He parked his car in the driveway and they went into the house, entering the kitchen through the back entrance. Vince made certain he locked the door behind them.

Leading her to the family room, he turned to BET's *106 & Park* on the 52-inch, flat screen plasma television. They sat so close their thighs touched.

"You want a Pepsi?" Vince asked.

"I didn't come over here for a Pepsi. You know what I came to do." Tameka flirted with Vince.

He smiled. "I like a shorty that knows what she wants."

He placed his hand on her leg and slowly moved it up her skirt. He kissed her neck as she began to moan. She smelled so good—like strawberries. Vince wanted to eat her up. She wrapped her arms around his neck and pulled him closer. In one fell swoop he managed to pull her shirt over her head, lay her back on the couch, and position himself on top of her.

The front door squeaked and opened.

"Ooooh, snap!" Vince said, jumping up and pulling Tameka with him. They headed for the hall closet, but he knew they wouldn't make it in time, so he dragged her behind the couch where they kneeled. Tameka's shirt lay on the floor where they had been sitting. Vince stretched his arm under the couch, but his fingertips were still a couple inches out of reach. Sweat appeared on his face as he heard the sound of his mother's heels against the hardwood floor. *We caught up. Mom's is gonna put a beat down on me for real!* He quickly took his cell phone out of his pocket and reached for the shirt, pulling it out of sight within seconds of his mother's entrance. Unfazed, Tameka rested her chin on her fist as if certain nothing would happen.

Mrs. McCloud entered the family room and looked around. "Vince?" she called out.

Vince's heart raced as they remained frozen. Tameka wasn't tripping because she had been in this awkward situation many times before.

"Vince? Are you home?" she yelled. "How many times do I have to tell them to turn off the doggone lights and television when they leave this house?" she questioned. "His car is outside so he must be up at the park." She scratched her head.

Kathy McCloud turned off the television, went to the kitchen and grabbed her lunch bag out of the refrigerator. After placing it on the table she went upstairs to her room.

"Should we run for it?" Tameka whispered without any emotion.

"No! Stay right here. She'll probably leave in a minute. Besides, the door would make too much noise," Vince responded.

Ten minutes passed before Mrs. McCloud descended the stairs. To Vince and Tameka, it seemed like an hour. Finally, she grabbed her lunch bag and left. As soon as she closed it, Vince's cell phone rang. He couldn't believe his bucked eyes and alert ears. His mother was probably calling to fuss at him for leaving the television on. Had she called while she was still in the house, he would've been busted.

Tameka fell over on her side and cracked up laughing. Vince chuckled along to hide his relief. Adjusting his pants, he realized he got some kind of charge from almost getting busted. He fell on top of Tameka and kissed her hard.

NINETY-NINE PROBLEMS

CHAPTER
8

C rea and Fiona walked out of the air-conditioned theater into the ninety-degree heat. The humid breeze that whooshed past them didn't supply any relief. Everyone exiting the show seemed to be discussing different movie scenes.

"I'm buying that movie as soon as it comes out on DVD. Mmm mm mm! Chris Brown and Columbus Short know they are too sexy. I'll *stomp the yard* with them any day!" Fiona fanned her face with her hand.

"You ain't never lied. That's definitely one for the collection." Crea shook her head in agreement.

"My baby got them faded on the body, though. Romero lifts weights every day. Girl, I love when he hugs me with those big strong arms." Fiona blushed and began laughing.

"Anyway!" Crea rolled her eyes. "I know Brandon would love that movie. He dances just like Chris Brown," she said.

"If I didn't know any better, I'd think you like Brandon." Fiona looked at Crea out the corner of her eye.

61

"Please! You know we're just cool. He's like my little brother."

"Then you must be committing incest in your mind because I know you like him as more than a friend, Crea. How long have I been knowing you?"

"Okay, okay, maybe a little, but it doesn't matter anyway. He still has a girlfriend." Crea shrugged.

"As much as you say they argue, they probably won't last too much longer. Then you'll be right there to snatch him up." Fiona winked.

"Girl, you're crazy." They both laughed. *I sure hope you're right,* Crea thought.

Crea pulled her lip gloss out her purse and brushed it across her lips. "Are we still going shopping? We need to find something to wear to the all-white dance, plus I need some cute flat shoes and accessories to go with the orange Deréon sundress I bought last week." Crea stumbled over a crack in the sidewalk.

Fiona grabbed her hand to stop her from falling. "Watch it, clumsy." She giggled. "I may not go to the dance."

"What you mean you're not going?" Crea stopped and stared at Fiona.

"Romero don't want to go to the dance, so I'm gonna hang out with him that night. But we can still go shopping."

Crea rolled her eyes and started walking away. She couldn't believe how Fiona was letting Romero control her every move. She wanted to shake some sense into her, but she just ignored the comment because she knew Fiona wouldn't change her mind anyway.

"My mom didn't give me but $20. You know how cheap she is. But I'm sure I'll find a hot top on sale. I should've asked Romero for some money before he left." Fiona adjusted her blue jean miniskirt for the tenth time.

The sidewalk was packed with pedestrians. Adults carried shopping bags while children struggled to keep up.

"Girl, the only reason I get to shop is because my mother gets social security checks for us since my dad died," Crea said, quickly getting off the subject of Romero. "She keeps some to help pay bills, but she gives us most of it. Dad even put money up for us to go to college, too. I guess he wanted to make sure we would be okay. Girl, I miss him so much, Fi." Crea took a deep breath and blew it out slowly.

"Yeah, I miss him, too. He was the closest thing I had to a father . . ." Her words trailed off as she squinted at a blue Chevy Blazer sitting at the light.

"Romero!" she shouted and began walking toward the vehicle driven by a three-hundred pound albino.

Romero sat on the passenger's side rocking his head to the music blasting from the truck's speakers. Two girls also sat in the back seat moving to the music. Romero passed the blunt to his boy and looked in Fiona's direction. "Man, pull over." He pointed to the nearest curb. His driver whipped over to the right and Romero hopped out of the SUV, fixing his white wife-beater and Sean John jeans. His usual 'fro was now braided up.

"Hey, shorty, what you doing down here?" Romero asked Fiona, whose narrowed brows gave her a confused expression.

"Me and Crea just came from the movies. So ummm, what are you doing down here? When I talked to you yesterday, you said you were going to Cleveland for the weekend."

"Sweetheart, don't even trip," he responded. "You're looking good in this mini." He gently tugged on the bottom of it and licked his lips.

Fiona ignored his comment. "And who are they?" Fiona pointed to the passengers in the back seat.

"They ain't nobody, baby." He pulled her into his arms and kissed her on the forehead.

"Hey, Romero, you can't speak?" Crea bucked her eyes. She didn't expect them to still be seeing each other after two months, but unfortunately they were. Fiona was already going through all kinds of drama with him, but she just wouldn't leave him alone. Whenever she came crying to Crea about something he did, she told her that he was no good, but Fiona would make excuses for him. Besides, Vince had already told her that Romero was a playboy, a gangbanger, and a weed head. But Fiona wasn't trying to hear that either.

Romero was supposed to be in his senior year at Fenton, despite the fact that he didn't attend school much. He could usually be found two blocks away, hanging in the park smoking weed with other 47th Street Dragons. But for some reason, he had Fiona wrapped around his finger.

"What's up, Crea?" he said, turning his gaze back to Fiona. "Baby, I gotta get going. I got some business to take care of, but I'll call you later. Here's a few dollars. Go buy yourself something nice." He pulled out a roll of money and handed her a $100 bill. He pulled his sagging pants up on his waist and headed back to the Blazer. Fiona took the money and put it in the front pocket of her miniskirt. Before she could look back up at him, he was opening the passenger door of the SUV.

"I'll call you later. Peanut, let's roll," he said to the driver as he slammed the door shut. The girls in the back seat smirked as they looked Crea and Fiona up and down while the SUV pulled into traffic.

Crea folded her arms as she and Fiona watched the Blazer merge into traffic. "That's it? All he has to say is that he has business to take care of?" Crea was fed up with the way Romero was treating Fiona. Placing one hand on her hip, she tilted her head to one side. "Why would he tell you he was going out of town? And who were those girls?"

Fiona shrugged. "I guess he changed his mind about going out of town. And those girls couldn't have been too important or else he wouldn't have pulled over and gave me money. Now let's go shopping." Fiona continued walking.

"Fi, he's a straight up dog. Why can't you see that? You *know* I'm telling you the truth. Not only does he lie, but he fakes you out all the time. You need to stop waiting around on him and *move on*."

"Crea, he's really not that bad. Girl, I got him sprung anyway. You see he's giving me money."

Crea's mouth hung open. "Sprung? Fiona Spencer, have you slept with him?"

"No, I haven't slept with him, but we have come close. I've thought about letting him be my first." A half-smile appeared across Fiona's face.

"Are you *serious*? You're thinking about giving up your virginity to *him*? I don't get you. He's a no-good, pot head dropout. You can do much better. Tell him to kick rocks and get you someone who'll treat you better."

"Everyone doesn't have plans to wait until they're married like you, Crea. I don't need you telling me what not to do with Romero. How you gon' tell me about my man when you don't even have one?" Fiona said, with her hand on her hip.

"Tuh! I'd rather be by myself than to put up with a dumb loser who wants to be a player. I'm just trying to be a friend, but if you like how he treats you, then that's on you." Crea stormed away in the opposite direction. She was tired of Fiona's drama with Romero and was no longer in the mood to shop. In fact, she wanted to get as far away from Fiona as possible.

Furious, Crea was walking so fast that sweat began to drip down her forehead. Wiping the sweat away, she turned the corner that led to the train station entrance. The blue Chevy Blazer pulled up and one of the girls from the back seat got out, followed by Romero. Crea stood off to the side so he wouldn't see her. She didn't want him asking about Fiona. He stood there hugging the girl's small waist and whispering something in her ear.

Crea shook her head. Romero pulled out his wallet and handed the girl some money. "Man, my daddy was right about everything."

Crea couldn't help but remember the day her dad busted her crushing on Vince's friend, Reggie. Every time he came over to hang out with Vince, Crea put on one of her favorite outfits and sat in the family room with them while the boys played the

Xbox, hoping Reggie would compliment her. One day Vince Sr. entered the room, glanced at the boys then at Crea.

"Come here, sweetheart," he said, turning to walk into the kitchen.

"Yes, Dad," Crea said, leaving the room. She glanced back to see if Reggie was watching, but his gaze was fixed on the TV. Sadly, she exhaled and took a seat next to her dad at the table.

"Nice outfit. Did you wear it just for me?" he asked.

Crea swallowed, trying to rid herself of the fear in her stomach as she nodded up and down.

"Well, I think you look great and I love you just the way you are." He grabbed her hand and gently squeezed it. "Crea, I don't want you thinking you need to dress a certain way to get some guy's approval. See, guys think they're slick. They'll say things to make you feel special—like you're the only girl for them—then still turn around and make a complete fool out of you in front of all of your friends and theirs, too."

The loud honking from an angry driver made Crea jump. *This had to be what he was talking about. In Fiona's eyes, Romero can do no wrong.* She glared at Romero as he slipped his tongue into the girl's mouth.

More agitated than ever, she took her cell phone out of her purse and set it on camera mode. Just as she looked back in their direction, Romero and the girl were kissing deeply. Crea started taking pictures.

"If Fiona doesn't wake up after this, then I'm through with it." She pressed the send button on her cell phone, forwarding the pictures to Fiona.

67

NINETY-NINE PROBLEMS

CHAPTER
9

Vince thought today would be the perfect opportunity to get Tameka back over to the crib. His mom had recently switched shifts, so she was up and gone before Vince's alarm sounded. He called Tameka on her cell last night.

"You gon' come hang out with me tomorrow?" Vince asked. "My moms will be at work."

"I can't, boo. I have a test to take tomorrow."

"Your teacher will let you make that up another day. I want to see you."

"I wanna see you too, but I can't tomorrow. This teacher don't play no make-up mess," Tameka smacked her lips.

"You sure I can't change your mind?" Vince pleaded.

"I can't, Vince," Tameka whined. "I'll make it up to you another day, okay babe?"

"Yeah, you better. Hit me up later," Vince said before hanging up.

It was almost time to leave for school. Vince knew he had to take Crea and Fiona, even if he didn't plan on staying. He

69

wasn't feeling classes, so he decided to call Marcus to see what he was on. Marcus cut school at least two times a week, so he always knew where the "cut-out" would be held. A group of kids took turns hosting cut-out parties. There would be no parental supervision, but lots of girls, alcohol, and video games. Most days were fine, but every once in a while things got out of hand. One day a neighbor called the police, and when they showed up, all twenty students ran to the back door, trying to escape. They had no clue that a patty wagon was waiting for them outside. Vince was glad he had an exam that day because he too would have been there.

"What up, man? Anybody having something at their crib today?" Vince asked when Marcus answered the phone.

"And you know this man..." Marcus said in his best Chris Tucker voice. "I have some business to take care of first so meet me in the parking lot after third period."

"Cool." They both hung up.

At 10:20 a.m. Vince met Marcus outside the school. They headed toward Marcus's car.

"Man, I still can't get that kid from the park out of my head. I've been tripping on that ever since it happened. He was just playing in the park, man. He didn't deserve to get shot down like that." Vince shook his head.

"Don't let it get to you, man. I ain't sayin' it ain't messed up, but you know how it is around here. That park is a war zone." Marcus opened his trunk, pulled out a towel, and started wiping his   06 Monte Carlo, custom painted midnight blue and sitting on twenty-twos.

"Man, Money, this is a nice ride."

"Yeah, this my baby here," Marcus said. "I gave my cousin $500 to put the title in her name.

"Dang, man, where you get that Rockefeller money? Somebody died in the fam' and left you some stacks?" Vince walked around Marcus's new car nodding his head.

"Yeah, right. All my fam' live in the 'jects. So if any of 'em had money to leave me, I'm sure they would've got out the ghetto a long time ago." Marcus smirked.

Vince thought about the rust stains on the passenger door of his car, the hanging rear bumper, and the cracking leather on his interior seats. Marcus was driving one of his dream cars and he couldn't help feeling a little jealous. He talked to his mom a few times about getting another car, but she told him if he wanted another one, he needed to get a job and save his money. Vince tried saving a few times, but once he saw a pair of gym shoes he liked, he didn't hesitate to purchase them with his savings.

"Man, if you come work with me, you can have a whip like this, too." Marcus pulled a wad of money out his pocket and began counting it.

"For real? I need a job. Can you hook me up?" Vince was excited about the thought of flossing a new car. "I know you're not still working at Pete's Pizzeria making that kind of loot, so where you at?"

"Naw, man. I wasn't making enough paper at Pete's. I work for Crazy Mike now. You know he's been trying to get you on his team for the longest. You want me to tell him you're ready so you can make some real money?"

The thought of riding in a fully-loaded, black-on-black Dodge Charger with a hot chick on the passenger side popped in

71

Vince's mind, quickly followed by the incident of Crazy Mike beating up his cousin.

"Crazy Mike! Money, have you lost your *mind*? Man, I saw that dude yesterday. You already know what he does to his workers if his money comes up short. If the man can beat his own blood over money, what you think he'll do to you? Man, you messing with fire."

Marcus hit the unlock button on his keychain remote. They hopped in and headed toward Dave's house.

"I've been working for Mike for a month and I'm his top seller. He gave me a $3,000 bonus the other day. I don't plan on getting on his bad side. I've been in the streets all my life. I know how the game is played. Besides, I got a son to feed. I can't have him out here wearing wack clothes and jumpers. You need to stop punkin' out and come make some of this cake." Marcus put the crisp dollars under his nose and inhaled.

"I ain't in the business of making all that for another stud. If I'm gonna be out here hustlin', it'll be for me. I just hope you know what you're doing."

"I got this. Quit actin' like a female," Marcus joked as he popped in 50 Cent's latest CD.

"Naw, you're the female. Crazy Mike's female," Vince cracked. They both laughed.

"Okay, Mr. Funny Man, you got me. I hope these fools got some food over here. I'm starving."

"Dude, I almost got busted the other day by moms. I had that shorty I met at McDonald's over to the crib yesterday and Moms popped up from outta nowhere."

"Straight up? That's funny."

"It wasn't funny at the time." Vince shook his head as he told the story.

"Maaan, yo' momma would've been all up in that butt if she would've caught y'all," Marcus cracked on Vince.

"Man, she would've straight up killed me."

"What did you say your shorty's name is?"

"Tameka."

"Tameka? How she look?"

"She's about my mom's complexion with a Halle Berry hair cut and a big onion."

"Does she stay over on Wood Street?" Marcus asked.

"Yeah. You know her?" Vince looked at him with a raised brow.

Marcus pulled his car in a spot right next door to Dave's two-flat brownstone. Marcus got out and stretched. Vince opened his door and sat on the edge of his seat with his feet on the curb, tying his blue and gold Air Max shoes that matched his T-shirt.

"So where you think you know her from?" Vince brought up the subject again.

Marcus was about to answer when he spotted an older woman tightly clutching her purse with one hand as she continued walking in their direction.

"Oh, snap! That's Dave's mom." Marcus grabbed his cell phone and typed: UR MOM IS COMIN UP DA BLOCK, and quickly pressed the send button.

Vince and Marcus got back in the car and waited to see what would happen next. Once David's mom stuck her key in the door and went inside, two minutes passed without a stir.

Suddenly, kids came rushing out. A lanky boy with braids had one shoe on and the other in his hand, followed by a short girl with a hotdog in her hand.

"Get your dumb behinds back to school and don't ever come back here again!" David's mom shouted at the top of her lungs as she swung a bat in the air. After the kids ran off, she slammed the door.

Vince and Marcus were laughing so hard, they didn't see the police cruiser pull up next to them. The driver was blonde with ocean-blue eyes. The other officer was an older black guy with a plump face and receding hair line. Both officers stared at them coldly. When the boys finally looked up, their facial expressions changed quicker than a yellow light turning red in the 'hood. The officers stepped out of their squad car with their right hands on their pistols strapped to their hip.

"I need you two to slowly step out of the vehicle, now!" the black officer said strongly as he moved toward the Monte Carlo.

Vince and Marcus slowly stepped out of the car with their hands in the air. Vince's body trembled. His heart raced uncontrollably. Marcus bit down on his jaws as he placed his hands on top of the hood.

"I need to see some identification, boys. What the hell are you doing around here at this time of day? Shouldn't you be in school? What? Looking to break into somebody's apartment? Where did you steal this car from, huh?" the long-faced officer questioned.

"Ain't nobody steal no car. Man, this my cousin's car. I'll give you her name and number so you can call and ask her," Marcus said with an attitude.

"*Man!* Who are you calling *man*? You address us as officer or sir. Do you hear me, boy? Officer Fat Face grabbed Marcus, forcing him around to face him. Marcus mean mugged him.

"Oh, I see, you wanna go for tough. You a gangster? What you represent?" He patted Marcus's pants pockets and felt the roll of money. He pulled it out and smiled at his partner.

"Hey, Jim, lunch is on Mr. Tough Guy today." They both laughed.

"Man, that's my dough. Give it back to me." Marcus tried to grab the money, but the officer punched him in the stomach, took out his baton, striking him all over his body. Marcus fell to the ground and curled up in a fetal position, hollering in agony. The other officer started kicking him in his back.

Vince stood frozen in shock. He didn't know if he should just stand there or run for his life. He started backing away from the car, looking for an escape route. Marcus appeared lifeless, but the cops didn't seem to care. As Vince got ready to make his move, the white officer turned around.

"Where do you think you're going?" He lunged at Vince with his baton, hitting him on the arm and the leg.

Vince dropped to the ground and covered his head with both hands. The blows were agonizing and felt like they were going to tear his flesh apart. He cried out for the officer to stop, but that seemed to only make him swing harder. Distant police sirens were approaching. Vince was afraid that more cops were on the way to join in on the beating. On television he'd seen situations like this, but never imagined it could happen to him.

Several seconds passed before a slamming door and clunky steps echoed against the pavement. "Kozlowski, Jefferson, get over here right now!" a short muscular officer in a white uniform shirt yelled. "What the hell are you doing out here in broad daylight? Someone phoned this in, so it's obvious you're being watched. You better hope you're not being videotaped, idiots. The ink is not even dry on the last lawsuit. What are you tryin' to do? Dig us in a hole we can't get out of?" His face turned beet-red as he spoke. "Let them go right now, and get your butts back to the station." He got back in his car, slammed the door and sped off.

"Today is your lucky day, boys. Get your butts outta here before I drag you down to the station," Kozlowski said.

Both cops strolled back to their vehicle, talking, laughing and giving high-fives like they had just finished watching a basketball game. Vince was in pain, but clearly not as much as Marcus. It took fifteen minutes to get him in the back seat of his car and that was only after a man coming down the street helped them. Vincent slowly climbed into the driver's seat, lifting one sore leg after another. He started the engine and drove to the nearest hospital.

Vince returned home later that night in pain and tears.

"Why are you walking like that, Vince? What happened to you?" Kathy frowned after seeing her son quietly limping past her toward the kitchen.

His entire body jerked at the sound of her voice. He wasn't expecting his mother to still be awake. Her new work shift usually had her in bed by 8 p.m. Slowly, he turned to face her. "Mom, what are you doing up?" He looked in the family room where she was sitting on the couch.

"I asked you a question. Why are you limping?"

Vince knew he had to come up with a lie because his mother would have a fit if she knew he had cut school. "Oh," he grunted. "I was at the park playing ball, and this big dude was guarding me. He knocked me down and my whole left side is bruised."

"Well, be careful out there. Maybe you should take a hot bath." She went back to writing out checks for her bills.

Vince got some ice cubes out the freezer, put them in a sandwich bag, and placed it on his right shoulder. He was furious at the way the police had beat him and Marcus like animals. He felt helpless. He knew there was no use reporting it. No one would believe him over the law. *What would Dad do if he were here?* he wondered.

Crea was on the stairs listening to their conversation. Vince wasn't in school that day and she thought there was something fishy about the story he'd told their mother. He was tripping all over his words like he was making the story up off the top of his head.

Later that night, she headed to his room to see if he would tell her what really happened. As she got closer, she heard what sounded like her brother arguing through sobs. She assumed he was on the phone.

"Dad, why did you leave me? You're supposed to be here for me. I got beat down today by Five-0 for *no reason*. I hate your guts, man!" Vince's cries suddenly ended.

Crea raised her fist to knock on his door, but slowly lowered it back to her side. She didn't remember seeing her brother cry at their father's funeral or any other time after his death. He always appeared stone-faced, like he wasn't even in the same

77

room. Now she knew for sure that he was in just as much pain as she had been. As much as she wanted to go in and hug her brother, she didn't want him to think she was snooping. Crea went back to her room and cried herself to sleep.

CHAPTER 10

Ever since that night she heard him in his room cursing their father for dying, Crea was extremely concerned about Vince. He hadn't been going out or even talking much, for that matter. And she couldn't figure out why he was so upset with their dad. She knew something was wrong because he hadn't cracked on her or pushed her around. The strangest change was him going to all his classes.

"I'm going to the freshman dance, Vince. Wanna go?" Crea popped her fingers and moved to an imaginary beat.

"What I look like going to a freshman dance?"

"To me, you'd look like Vince Jr.," she said plainly.

"Anyway, I'm geeked. Ready to get my dance on," she said, slow dancing her way out of the living room.

Vince waved her away, looking irritated.

Crea stopped and turned to look back at Vince. "So what are you gonna do? Momma is at work picking up extra hours."

"Chill with this lil' hottie that I'm talking to," he said without an expression.

"Be careful," Crea said. "You know what Dad said about having sex—"

"Chill wit' all that. Seriously, I don't wanna hear it."

"Sorry," she said, regretting that she'd brought up their dad. Her cell phone rang and she answered right away. "Hello?"

"It's jukin' time, heyyyy," Lela said into the phone.

Crea was forced to smile and shake her head.

"Girl, I'm looking so hot the boys won't know what to do with all of me. See you in a few. I'm on my way," Lela said.

"Okay, I'll be ready."

"You better be. Deuces."

"Okay, bye." Crea ended the call.

Although Vince was still in a foul mood, Crea had to admit she was excited about the freshman dance. She had the perfect shoes to go with the perfect outfit. Her crisp, white linen pants hugged her lower body and stopped just above her open toe, wedge-heeled sandals. Her matching top flowed a little past her hips, and a large belt embraced her flat stomach. The only thing missing was Fiona. They had not spoken since the incident with Romero a week ago.

After Crea forwarded the picture of Romero kissing another girl, she'd hoped Fiona would see his true colors. He was a dog, plain and simple. But when Fiona finally responded, she told Crea she needed to get her a man so she could stop worrying about hers. All Crea could do was gasp then scream, "Oooh, she's so stupid! Arghhhh!"

Romero had told Fiona he snapped on the girl that kissed him, telling her not to get their friendship twisted. And Fiona believed him. Crea and Fiona had never gone a day without talking, let alone a week. But they both were acting like stubborn mules, waiting on the other to call. This allowed Crea to get somewhat closer to Lela.

Lela was cool, but she could be a bit 'extra'—the word Crea and Fiona used to describe her over-the-top personality. Normally, Crea would have had Vince take them to and from the party, but after the police incident, he didn't do much driving.

At 8 P.M., Lela's mother dropped them off in front of the school gym where the party was being held. It looked like the red carpet at the BET Awards. One group even rented a stretch Hummer limo for the occasion. All the attendees were styling and profiling for the cameras.

"Okay, you two meet me right here at 11:30," Lela's mother said as the girls got out the car.

"Yes mother. We heard you the other three times." Lela slammed the front passenger door and rolled her eyes.

Crea looked at Lela like she was crazy. If she even tried to get sassy with her mother, she would be picking up her teeth off the ground. Crea was unable to see Lela's outfit in the car, but now that she had, she was ashamed to walk with her. Lela wore a white denim miniskirt, showing cottage-cheese-looking cellulite on the back of her legs. Her cotton halter top made her look like she was harboring two baby watermelons. People stared and whispered as she walked by, but according to Lela, "They either love my style or they're some haters."

As they walked into the gym the music was blasting and the dance floor was already packed. Teachers and other chaperones were on guard to break up any fights or freaky dancing that might occur. A huge balloon arc sat near the entrance for everyone to walk through. *They really went all out*, Crea thought.

"This is my jam!" Lela hollered as she moved from side to side and snapped her fingers.

"It's packed in here. And I see a lot of folks that *claimed* they weren't coming," Crea said, looking around the room. Surprised by the scene in front of her, Crea did a double take when she saw Fiona and Romero standing near the punch bowl. A part of Crea was happy to see Fiona, but since Romero was with her, she refused to approach her.

Fiona unexpectedly turned her way. They locked eyes. All the anger Crea felt washed away in an instant. She just wanted her best friend back. Crea couldn't be sure, but Fiona seemed to have a slight smile on her face. When Romero noticed her gaze focused across the room, he turned to see what had her attention. Once he spotted Crea, he grabbed Fiona's forearm and turned her toward him.

"I'm about to hit the dance floor. Are you coming or what?" Lela asked, moving to the beat of the music.

"Huh? What? Did you say something?" Crea asked, now facing Lela.

"I said are you going to dance?"

"Oh, no. Go ahead. I'll catch up with you later." Crea was glad to escape the stares that came their way. Thirsty and craving a Pepsi, she headed to the concession stand. Someone hugged her from behind, gently locking her arms at her sides. She jerked and tried to turn around but couldn't.

"Dag, Cee, you look good in white, girl," Brandon said as he let her loose. "You got your hair laid and your make up on. Who you trying to impress?" he said, noticing everything about her once she turned to face him.

"Boy, you almost got knocked out coming up behind me like that."

"I could've picked you up and carried you away and you would've been defenseless."

"Whatever, man." She looked Brandon up and down in his white linen pants suit and all white classic Reeboks. "Wow, you look nice yourself. I've never seen you wear anything but jeans. How does it feel to dress like a mature young man for once?" Crea joked.

"Why would I dress up just to come to school every day? Believe me, I got nice gear. I just wear them on the weekends."

"So, where is your shadow?" Crea laughed as she looked behind Brandon. "I know she can't be too far away."

"Actually, Alyssa's not here." His voice lowered slightly. "I took your advice and told her how I felt. And as you probably already know, she didn't take it well."

"What did she say?"

"She twisted every word I said. Talkin' 'bout, I just want to see other females. She told me too many guys wanted to get with her so I could push on. We argued for about thirty minutes before I said forget it."

"Oooh, maaan. You okay? I really thought if you were honest with her, she'd understand." Briefly she placed her hand on his right arm.

"It's cool. To tell you the truth, I was tired of fighting with her every other day. She's fine, but she's full of drama. I'm glad to finally let it go. I wanted to do it a long time ago, but my boys said I would be crazy if I did."

Crea felt a hint of jealousy when Brandon called Alyssa fine. She couldn't understand why these strong feelings she had for Brandon wouldn't go away. He looked so good tonight and she couldn't help thinking of him as more than just her friend.

"Hello!" Brandon waved his hand in front of Crea's eyes. "Did you hear me?"

"No. What did you say?" Crea snapped out of her thoughts.

"Do you think I should have left Alyssa a long time ago?"

"What difference does it make?"

"Just answer the question, Cee. Have I been looking like a fool all this time?"

"I wouldn't say all that. I just thought all the fighting was a sign that maybe you two weren't meant to be together. But that's just my opinion." Crea shrugged her shoulders and glanced around the room.

"Why didn't you tell me?"

"Tell you what? To dump your girlfriend? That wasn't for me to say."

Brandon's friend, Sean, walked over. He was known as the finest freshman in school. His wavy brown hair extended past his shoulders while brown freckles marked his face. Sean rubbed the little hair on his chin as he looked Crea up and down.

"Hey, Crea, you lookin' good, girl. You should let me take you out sometime."

Brandon jumped in real quick. "Sean, man, chill. Where's your girl, Tiffani?"

Crea wasn't sure, but she could swear that Brandon was jealous. She smirked.

"B, why you blockin'?" Sean questioned.

"I ain't blockin'. I'm just sayin' . . ." Brandon didn't know what to say. He didn't like Sean trying to talk to Crea. It wasn't just because Sean was known as a player around school because he could just give Crea the 4-1-1 on him anytime. Brandon realized he had feelings for Crea and they were more than just in a sisterly way. Brandon always thought she was cute and had even thought about asking her out in the beginning. But once they became close friends, she told him her mother didn't want her dating yet, so he didn't bother asking. But with Alyssa out of the picture, he could at least tell her how he felt.

"Sean, *please*. You've messed with two girls in my health class at the same time. You had them in there about to fight. Thanks, but I think I'll pass on that date." Crea smiled.

"You sure? I'll cut all the other females off just for you," Sean answered smoothly.

"I'm probably going to miss out on a good thing, but I'll still have to pass," Crea said sarcastically.

Crea could have sworn she saw smoke coming from his ears. Sean was not used to being turned down. When Crea looked at Brandon, she noticed a satisfied smirk on his face. He always made comments about guys who had tried to talk to her, but she always thought he was playing the little brother role. Now that she thought about it, he never had anything nice to say about *any* of the guys she showed an interest in. They were never good enough.

"Sean, Tiffani's over there trying to get your attention, man." Brandon pointed to a girl in a long, strapless dress.

Sean turned around and smiled. "I'll get wit' y'all later."

Brandon pointed at Sean. "Can you believe him? I already told him before not to try to holler at you. All he does is mess females around. You gotta be careful who you mess with up here. They'll put your business on blast in the locker room, and the next day the whole school knows about it."

Crea wasn't mistaken about Brandon. He was clearly jealous. He always played this protective role with her when it came to guys. She now realized it wasn't because he was playing the brother role. Crea believed he really liked her. But, she wouldn't call him on it. He would have to tell her. Her father always taught her that the guys should approach the girl.

She folded her arms across her chest. "Is that right? So are there any nice guys here at Fenton that you think are okay to kick it with? You kind of make it sound like everyone is a dog but you."

Brandon scratched the side of his head. He was nervous. This was an opportunity to come clean with Crea, but he didn't know how she would take it. Would something like this destroy their friendship? He didn't want to lose her as a friend, so he decided not to tell her, at least not yet.

"Well, I am the best candidate, but since you're my big sister . . ." He dusted off his shirt, quickly glancing at Crea.

"Yeah, too bad." The last thing she wanted to hear him call her was 'big sister,' but she played it off with a grin.

"So, are you going to dance with me or what? It's not like you have a date or anything," Brandon joked.

"Ha-ha. You want to dance now? This is a slow song," Crea said, referring to one of Usher's old ballads.

"So what, you think I stink or something?"

"Shut up, Brandon." She grabbed his hand and led him to the dance floor.

Brandon hugged Crea around the waist. She held him around his neck and rested her head on his shoulder. She took a deep breath and imagined him kissing her lips softly. Brandon felt electricity flowing through his body as he held her close. Her being in his arms felt so right and he never wanted the song to end.

I gotta tell her. I gotta let her know I'm feeling her. This little brother thing ain't gonna fly. Brandon's thoughts were going haywire. Just as he was about to whisper how he felt in her ear, the song ended and his nerves were shot down.

As they walked off the dance floor, Crea spotted her real brother.

"Say, what are you doing here?" she asked. "I thought you didn't do freshman dances."

"I don't, but I was bored, so I thought I'd grace y'all with my presence," Vince said as he brushed his fade.

"Dude, no one would've missed your so-called *presence*," Crea said.

"Can you believe this, man? My own sister is a hater." His response made Crea's eyes brighten. It was good to see some of the old Vince in action.

Brandon laughed. "Y'all crazy."

Vince tapped Crea's shoulder once. "Hey, ain't that Fi over there?"

"Yeah, that's her," Crea said as she rolled her eyes.

"Y'all still ain't talking?"

"Nope. And I ain't about to kiss her butt. All I tried to do was tell her about that jerk and she played me for him."

"Man, this is stupid. Y'all been friends for too long to be up in here acting like y'all don't know each other." Vince walked toward Fiona, tired of the ridiculous feud between her and Crea. He approached the table where Fiona and Romero were sitting.

"What up, Fi? Can I holler at you for a minute?"

"Dude, what you need to talk to my girl about? She ain't goin' nowhere." Romero stood in front of Fiona, blocking Vince from speaking to her.

"Let's just go, Romero," Fiona pleaded as she tugged on his left arm.

"Man, I ain't even talkin' to you." Vince stepped in his face. "Fiona is like a baby sister to me."

"Well, she don't need your protection, *big brother*, so I think you better head back over to the other side of the room. I got this over here." Romero stared Vince in the eyes as his wide nose flared.

Crea and Brandon walked up behind Vince. "Come on, Vince, man. It's not worth it," Brandon said.

"Yeah, let's just go," Crea said, grabbing her brother's arm.

88

"You better listen to 'em, partner, before you get stomped."

Vince shoved Romero, pushing him back into Fiona. Romero swung his right fist at Vince's face but missed.

Mr. Mercer ran over to them and stopped the commotion. "What the heck is going on here? Everyone get back to dancing before I stop this party. Now!" he told the crowd.

As they dispersed, leaving Vince, Brandon, and Crea on one side and Romero and Fiona on the other, Mr. Mercer asked what the problem was.

"We good. Ain't that right, *big brother?*" Romero said as he glared at Vince.

"Whatever, dude. Those looks don't scare me."

"We'll see. Fiona, let's go. Now!" Romero said as he grabbed Fiona by the wrist.

"You don't have to go with him if you don't want to. I can take you home." Vince stared at Fiona, but she wouldn't look at him.

"Man, you really tryna' set it off up in here." Romero let Fiona go and stepped toward Vince.

Mr. Mercer blocked him, placing his hand up to Romero's chest. "It's over, Romero. Just leave before things get out of hand."

"I'm good, Vince. Really. Let's go, Romero." Fiona grabbed his arm.

"It's cool. I'm out. But I'll see you around, homey," Romero said to Vince as he walked backwards, staring at him with a smirk on his face.

"Dude, I ain't worried."

Mr. Mercer was trying to keep things from getting out of hand. He didn't want any of the other chaperones to see what was going on. He also didn't want Vince getting into any more trouble.

"Vince, what are trying to do? Get kicked out of school?" Mr. Mercer asked.

"I just came over here to talk to Fiona. He's the one tryin' to boss up." Vince looked Romero up and down as his lip quivered.

Mr. Mercer spoke in his ear, trying to get through to him. "You have to try to avoid situations like these. Guys like him don't fight fair."

"I ain't shook."

"Stop being hot-headed and listen to what I'm *saying!*" Mr. Mercer cursed. "It's not like when I was coming up. We fought with our fists. Today, they use guns and knives. I just don't want to see anything happen to you. Your mother would be devastated."

"Yeah, well maybe I got something for him, too. I gotta go." He turned to leave with Crea following behind him.

Mr. Mercer took a deep breath and shook his head. *Vincent, my friend, I'm trying my best to get your son on the right path. This young man . . . I don't know, man. I just don't know about this generation.*

CHAPTER
11

After last night's drama at the all white dance, Crea didn't feel much like doing anything. She just wanted to sleep the day away. The altercation between Vince and Romero had her worried. If anything happened to her brother, she'd never forgive herself.

Crea and Vince stepped out of their rooms at the same time, both moving at a snail's pace.

"What a party, huh?" Crea shook her head.

"Man, that Romero dude thinks somebody is supposed to be scared of him. I want a piece of him so bad, I can taste it." Vince balled his fists and bit down on his jaws.

"Vince, I don't think you should mess with Romero. He doesn't seem like the type to fight fair," Crea pleaded with her eyes, genuinely scared for her brother.

"Well, I don't fight fair either. He better be worried about me and that's for real. I don't understand what Fiona sees in him. Is she smokin' and y'all just didn't tell me?" Vince sarcastically questioned.

"I don't know. It's like he has her brainwashed or something," Crea said.

"Let's go, you two," Mrs. McCloud shouted from the kitchen.

Today was her father's forty-third birthday and her mother wanted to put flowers on his grave. They made visits to the cemetery three times a year—on her father's birthday, her parents' anniversary, and on Father's Day.

Crea turned to Vince. "I really don't see the purpose of going to the cemetery. I talk to Dad every day right in my room. Besides, if Dad's in heaven looking down on us, why are we even wasting our time talking to an empty grave?" she fussed.

"I'm not feeling this either," Vince agreed.

"And every time I ask Mom why we have to keep going to the cemetery if Dad's in heaven, all she says is, 'Don't question God.' How is that questioning God?" Crea threw her hands in the air and shrugged.

"Yeah, I hear you. It really doesn't make sense at all," Vince reasoned as they headed down the stairs.

Vince, Crea, and their mother, rode in silence to the cemetery. They entered the gate and turned right, passing by hundreds of headstones before reaching Mr. McCloud's. Once Mrs. McCloud parked, she and Crea opened their doors to get out, but Vince didn't move.

"Vince, grab the flowers," his mother ordered.

"I'm staying in the car, Ma." Vince slid further down in the back seat, closing his eyes, and resting his head on the leather cushion.

"What? Boy, get your butt out of this car, now!"

"For what? If he would've taken care of his health, he would still be here. All this running back and forth to talk to the dirt ain't about nothin'," Vince said calmly.

In two seconds, Mrs. McCloud reached Vince and slapped him with all her strength. Vince popped up in shock, holding his hand over his right cheek. He couldn't believe his mother had just slapped him.

"Don't you *ever* disrespect your father again as long as you live!"

Crea stood silent, biting her nails. She had never seen her mother so upset.

"No disrespect meant, but Ma, it is what it is. Dad complained about headaches all the time, but he hated going to the doctor. Had he listened to you when you told him to make an appointment all those times, maybe we wouldn't be here," Vince shouted back.

"Death is a part of life, Vince. Your father's dying is not his fault. He loved us. He wouldn't have purposely neglected his health. I know you're hurt, but don't blame your dad. Maybe you need to talk to someone about your feelings," Mrs. McCloud said, her voice cracking as tears streamed down her face.

"Can we just do this and get it over with? I have things to do." Vince climbed out of the car and headed to his father's tombstone.

Mrs. McCloud didn't know what to do with her son, but she didn't feel like dealing with his negative attitude now. She placed fresh lilies on her husband's gravesite while Crea and Vince stood a few feet away.

NINETY-NINE PROBLEMS

"Crea, I remember you crying to your father when kids made fun of your name. When your father told you your name's significance, your face just lit up," Mrs. McCloud said through a sad smile as more tears dripped down her cheeks.

Smiling at that memory, Crea tried to keep tears from falling. Soon, she and her mother stood around laughing at their favorite memories while Vince texted friends. He refused to participate.

Crea read a poem for her father and found herself looking down, then up, then down again, confused as to where her father's body really resided. *Heaven or the grave? Where is my dad? I'm confused,* she thought. Minutes later they had their moment of silence as they always did right before leaving. Crea closed her eyes and spoke to her father.

Dad,

Fiona didn't come today. She's never missed coming out here with us. I wish you were here to tell me what to do. This guy Romero has some type of spell over her or something. I really miss her, but I don't know how to handle this. Everything's so different between us now. I bet if you were here to talk to her, she'd listen. And Vince is cutting school and hanging out with the wrong crowd. I know he wouldn't even be trying that mess if you were here. He's driving Mom insane. Maybe you can come to him in a dream or something and get him on the right track. Oh, and I like this boy at school named Brandon, but I don't know how to tell him. I know, don't worry, no boyfriends yet.

When she finished talking to her dad, she stretched, feeling a sense of relief wash over her. After staying at the cemetery for forty-five minutes, they drove back home.

As Crea sat in the front seat of the car, she thought about Brandon. He had called her last night and they talked for over an hour about the drama at the dance and Brandon's relationship with Alyssa. She replayed some of their conversation in her head.

"Hey Crea, you busy?" Brandon had asked.

"Naw, I'm just laying here listening to my iPod. What's up with you?"

"It's official now. I did it," Brandon said.

"Did what? Or am I supposed to read your mind?" she had asked sarcastically.

"I broke up with Alyssa. I mean, I told her we were done for good."

"I thought you guys were already broken up?" Crea sat up in her bed and leaned against the headboard.

"She called and wanted to work things out, but I'm just tired of the same old drama. She didn't try to change anything about herself. Truthfully, besides her good looks, there's not much else to her. She acts like a ditzy blonde most of the time," Brandon complained.

"You two will probably be back together tomorrow," Crea said, although deep down she was hoping they wouldn't.

"Naw, we're through for good. Besides, I like someone else."

Crea's heart dropped. "Already, Brandon? Dang! It hasn't been a full twenty-four hours and you're on to another chick?"

"Naw, it's not all of a sudden. I've been liking this girl for a long time. I just never told her."

"You really move fast, don't you?" Crea was crushed. She had never gotten around to telling Brandon how she felt about him.

"I wanted to tell her at the dance, but I didn't know how she'd respond."

Crea's heart started racing. Brandon was with her all night. Could he be talking about her? "Sooooo, who is she?" she asked slowly.

"It's you, Crea. I'm tired of playing the lil' brother role. I'm feelin' you and I hope this doesn't mess up our friendship, but I've been liking you for a long time." Brandon stopped rambling to see how Crea would respond. "Aren't you going to say something?" he asked when she didn't speak.

"Wow, I just wasn't expecting that," she stated, still in shock.

Brandon took a deep breath. "It's cool. If you're not feelin' me, we're still friends."

"No, it's not that. I've liked you since the first day of school."

"What? All this time and neither of us said anything? That's funny." They both laughed.

"But Brandon, I don't want to hold you back. You know I can't have a boyfriend yet."

"What if I told you that I like you enough to wait until you can? But if I wait, you'll have to promise that I'll be your first date."

"I can do that," Crea responded with a big Kool-Aid smile.

Crea walked in her room and went straight to the nightstand. She picked up her cell phone to see if she had any missed calls. Her mom had a rule that all cell phones stayed home to avoid any interruptions while at the cemetery, but Vince couldn't have cared less.

When Crea flipped her phone open, six missed calls were displayed on the screen. She hit the view button. Two calls were from Brandon and the other four were from Fiona. She couldn't believe it. Maybe missing the gravesite visit made Fiona feel guilty.

This past week of not talking to Fiona felt more like a month and Crea missed her friend so much. They had been through so much together, good and bad. She was still upset at Fiona, though, for choosing Romero over her and had second thoughts about calling her back. Romero treated Fiona like some gum stuck to the bottom of his shoe. He bought her nice things, but it was always *after* he didn't show up for a date or *after* she'd caught him in a lie. Crea didn't think Fiona should allow him to mistreat her just because he gave her money.

Startled by the vibrating phone in her hand, Crea looked at the caller-ID. It was Fiona's home phone number. She let it ring four times before answering.

"Hello," she said dryly.

"Crea, can you come over, please?" Fiona said through sniffles.

"What? Girl, I haven't heard from you in a whole week and now you want me to up and run over there. Sorry, I have plans," she said. Anger made her miss the trembling in Fiona's voice.

"Cee, please, I need you." Fiona let out a loud cry. "I don't know what to do."

"What's wrong?" she said when she heard the urgency in her voice. "Are you okay? You're scaring me." Crea's heart thumped against her chest.

"Please, just come over."

"Okay, I'm on my way." Crea slipped her sandals back on. She didn't know what was going on, but her eyes were watering at the thought of something bad happening to her best friend. *I bet that no-good Romero broke up with her.* Crea's thoughts raced through her head. Whatever was going on, all she knew was that she needed to go see about her friend.

She rushed out the door. Fiona only lived four blocks away, but Crea felt like it was several miles. Running until she couldn't catch her breath, she slowed her pace to a light jog. When Crea reached the door of Fiona's building, she rang the bell and stepped back to look up at the third floor window.

"Who is it?" Fiona said in a weak tone.

"It's me. Crea. Buzz me in."

Crea swung the door open and ran up the stairs, taking them two at a time. The apartment door was slightly ajar so she walked in, closed the door behind her, and rushed to Fiona's room. She came to an abrupt stop when she saw Fiona's bruised face.

"Oh my goodness!" Crea gasped. "Who did this to you? Did you get jumped?" She sat next to Fiona on the edge of the bed.

Fiona grabbed Crea into a bear hug and cried in her arms. Crea held her friend tight and cried with her.

"He . . . he . . . he . . ." Fiona tried telling her what happened, but her words were scrambling all together and Crea couldn't understand her.

Easing out of Fiona's embrace, Crea said, "Slow down and tell me what happened."

"He . . . ra . . . ra . . . raped me!" Fiona said, placing her head back on Crea's shoulder and crying some more.

Crea's eyes bucked. "What! Did you say you were raped?"

Fiona shook her head yes.

"Oh my God! Did you tell your mom? Where's Ms. Spencer?"

"She had to work overtime. She's been working overtime like crazy for the past three months. We haven't really talked all that much."

"Fi, we need to go to the hospital or the police station." Pulling her cell phone out of her pocket, Crea said, "I'm going to call Vince and tell him to take us." Her hands shook as she dialed his number.

Fiona grabbed the phone out of Crea's hand. "No, you can't tell anyone about this or they may have me killed."

"Who are *they*, Fiona? What do you mean 'they may have you killed?' Who did this to you?"

"Romero," she cried out.

"That no good dog!" Crea shouted. "Oooo wee, I'ma find somebody to . . ."

"We were making out on his bed. He started unzipping my pants and I told him to stop because it was going too far. I told him I wasn't ready to have sex, but he said I owed him for all the money he gave me. His mother came in the room after he raped me and I begged her to help me."

"What did she do?" Crea asked.

"She called me a liar and told me if I went to the police, she'd have me taken care of." Fiona was hysterical. "I can't go to the police, Crea. I can't."

"Oh my goodness! Okay, okay, we'll figure out something." Crea took a deep breath and exhaled loudly.

After several minutes of silence Fiona said out of the blue, "He tried to call me right before you got here, but I didn't answer my phone."

"Who? Romero? He called you after what he did?" Crea snatched Fiona's phone off the bed. Sure enough his number was displayed under Missed Call. There was also an image of an envelope, indicating that a voice message was left. She pressed the open button to listen.

"Fiona, its Romero. I just wanted to see if you made it home okay. Give me a call. I hope you ain't still mad at me. Anyway, call me. Maybe I'll take you shoppin' tomorrow to make it up to you. Plus, you really didn't get a chance to meet my moms. Well, not technically. She really wanna get to know you. Call me back, Fi."

"That *dog*!" Crea shouted. "He's gonna pay for what he did to you."

"Seriously, Crea, I couldn't believe Romero's hood rat momma. She was actually smokin' a blunt when she walked in on us and blew the smoke right in my face when I asked for her help. She was even dressed like someone our age and was blinged up just like a real gangster."

Crea frowned. "She can get it, too."

"No, Crea. I just want to forget it ever happened. I wish I could just go back . . . I never would have talked to him. Never."

"Don't blame yourself. We'll have to figure out something," Crea said, her mind filled with images of revenge.

NINETY-NINE PROBLEMS

CHAPTER 12

Vince cursed and screamed. The previous night he began experiencing a burning sensation when he urinated. He knew it was some type of STD. Although he'd never had one, he'd heard stories from his friends about them. He only hoped and prayed that it wasn't HIV or AIDS, or even herpes like one of his homeboys had gotten.

Last week he had hooked up with Tameka again. That was the fifth time having her over to his house. After the first time he could tell Tameka wasn't new to the game. She was doing things to him no female had ever done and he had been with quite a few girls. He planned on hooking up with her again until he started having a burning feeling. He remembered Marcus telling him about a similar situation he'd had with a hood rat off his block, so Vince decided to call and ask him what he should do.

I hope Marcus pick up the phone, Vince thought as he pressed the last digit.

"Speak," Marcus answered.

"Man, what's up? How you doing, man?" Vince asked.

"Still a little sore. My breathing is off a little from the bruised ribs, but I been getting around a little better. I'm tired of being in this house, though. It's been a week straight and I feel like the walls are closing in on me. Plus, I need to get back out here and make my money."

Vince laughed. "I know it's killing you to be on lockdown at the crib."

"True that. You know something is up when I'm ready to go back to school," Marcus shook his head.

"Most definitely. But, check this out. I need to ask you something and I don't need *no* jokes," Vincent said. "I think I'm burning, man. I feel like I got fire shooting out my stuff." He frowned.

"Ha ha ha. Deg, you got caught up? Man, didn't I teach you not to mess around without a condom? You don't listen, playboy. Who got you? That chick, Michelle?"

"Naw, ol' girl Tameka I was telling you about. I never thought she was burning. Man, she was working me so good, I wasn't even thinking about a condom. She don't seem like the nasty type. She's always clean and smelling good. That body is out of this world. Marcus, man, believe me when I say, she is on point. A ten!" Vincent grinned.

"Well, you see where tens get you. You can't smell or look at a chick and tell if she's burning or not. So you need to use protection *every time*, and I do mean *every time*. I tried to tell you that day outside David's house that I think I know Tameka."

"Yeah, from where?"

"She used to mess with Mike's boy, JD. And word is, she burnt him."

Vince shook his head. "Man, that's messed up. I wish I would've known that before I touched her."

"After that time I got burnt, I quit sleeping with these females without strapping. Besides, I already got one shorty, so I don't need no more females talkin' 'bout I'm they baby daddy. I already got to deal with Treyvon's crazy momma every time I wanna see him. My brother got six kids by five chicks and he's only twenty-three. I ain't tryna be like him."

"Yeah, I feel you. I definitely don't want no shorties. But anyway, I need to go take care of this. What clinic did you go to?" Vince asked.

"I went to the county. They gon' take care of you, but be ready to sit down there all day. They real slow," Marcus replied. "But hit me up when you get back. I need to get out this house for a little while."

"Yeah, okay. I'm out." Vince hung up the phone and rushed to the clinic.

"*Remember son, always use protection. You don't want to catch something you can't get rid of.*" His father's voice of reason popped in his head too little too late. The damage had already been done.

Why didn't I listen? Vincent thought sadly. "Man, I need you here, Dad," Vince said almost desperately. "I miss you, man! I'm messing up everything!"

After sitting in the clinic waiting area for over three hours, Vince was finally called in the room to see a physician. A petite Asian nurse took his blood pressure and temperature then handed him a gown to change into. He changed, hopped on the examination table and waited for the doctor. When he entered, Vince was surprised at how young he looked, maybe ten years older than himself. He was Vince's complexion, about two inches taller with a nice fade and some fresh jumpers.

"How you doing? I'm Dr. Wright. What brings you in today?" The doctor asked as he washed his hands.

"I'm umm... umm... having this burning every time I pee," Vince stalled.

"Okay. Any pain or swelling?

"Naw, just the burning."

Dr. Wright slipped on a pair of rubber gloves and looked at Vince. "I need you to stand and hold your gown up so I can examine you."

Vince hesitated. He slowly got off the table and raised his gown. His body grew tense as Dr. Wright began lifting, poking and squeezing down there. After the exam, he sent Vince to the bathroom to urinate in a cup so he could send it to the lab to be tested for STDs. The doctor left the room and returned thirty minutes later with the results.

"Well, Vince, you have gonorrhea. Lucky for you, it's curable. I'm going to give you some medication. Make sure you take it until it's all gone. You also need to tell your partner or partners they need to see their doctor right away," Dr. Wright said as he wrote the prescription.

Vince avoided the doctor's eyes as he shook his head. He knew that it had to be a STD, but hearing the results made him feel ashamed and angry at the same time.

"Vince, I get guys in here like you every day— young and reckless. Every time you have unprotected sex you're putting yourself in danger of catching something you can't get rid of."

"I just don't feel the same with that plastic it on, doc."

"You may be right, but what would you rather do? Put a condom on and have sex or live with HIV or AIDS? Don't think it can't happen to you. In fact, last week, I had to tell a fifteen year old that he has HIV. He's been sexually active since the age of thirteen and ran into the wrong one. That's all it takes, man." Dr. Wright handed him the prescription and a small box of condoms. "I hope I don't see you back in here, Vince. Be smart," he said, then walked out the room.

Vince stood there thinking about what the doctor just told him. It never entered his mind once that he could contract HIV or AIDS until he was burning. He was shaken at the thought and knew he had to stop taking risks. Vince got dressed and had the prescription filled at the pharmacy down the hall, which took yet another hour. Glad that the worst was over, he hopped in his car and drove home.

Vince jumped in the shower, and ten minutes later he was dressed in some long denim shorts and a red T-shirt. He hadn't eaten since morning and his stomach was growling out of control. Vince called Marcus to let him know he was on his way, but didn't get an answer. If Marcus didn't call back within thirty minutes, Vince was heading out alone.

Nearly forty minutes later, Vince walked two blocks to Wendy's restaurant when his cell phone rang.

"What up? You ready to roll?" Marcus asked.

"Man, I'm a block away from Wendy's so you can meet me up there. I called you a half hour ago and waited around like some female or something."

"Whatever, man. I had to meet with Crazy Mike. I'll tell you about it when I get there."

"Should you be driving already?" Vince questioned Marcus.

"I'm good."

Vince placed his food order. Three minutes later, he found a table, sat down and quickly unwrapped his food. He bit into his burger, nearly swallowing it whole. By the time Marcus arrived, Vince was finished eating.

Marcus took a seat across from him and gave him some dap. Vince noticed the dark shades immediately. "Man, what's up with the sunglasses? The sun ain't even out right now. I thought you said you were too fine to wear shades." Vince laughed.

Slightly pulling his glasses down, Marcus peeked over the top. His left eye was purple and as big as a golf ball.

Vince almost rose from his seat, but half-covered his mouth instead. "Daaaang, man. What happened to your eye? You got jumped by Five-0 again?"

"Naw, man. I got a violation for coming up short the other day. Crazy Mike had to do what he had to do. He said me being in the hospital was no excuse. It's cool, though. I handled mine. He said he hated to do it, but the rules apply to everybody. I can't do nothing but respect him for that. I just gotta make sure I hustle harder."

"Money, what are you saying, man? It's cool to get muffed? Man, Crazy Mike don't care about you. He'll kill you over a missing dollar." Vince moved his hands while he spoke.

Marcus shrugged his shoulders. "Vince, it's cool, man. I can handle it. I make more sales than all his other guys, even the ones who been there for years. Besides, if I don't work, I don't eat and my son don't eat. I got a plan and it's foolproof. I'll be his right hand man in less than a year. I'ma stack my paper for about a couple years, then I'ma get out the game."

Vince sighed and shook his head. He knew there was no getting through to Marcus. His boy didn't see a life outside the drug game. "A'ight, man. Just watch your back."

NINETY-NINE PROBLEMS

CHAPTER
13

Crea missed the outgoing, spunky Fiona. The rape stole her spirit and kept her depressed most of the time. She and Crea could be laughing about something and then at the drop of a hat Fiona would start crying uncontrollably. Crea was the only one who really knew what happened and Fiona swore her to secrecy. Even Fiona's mother didn't know about the rape. When she asked about the bruises on her face, Fiona told her some girls from another neighborhood had jumped her.

A month had passed since that dreadful day when Romero violated her, but Fiona still struggled to push the incident behind her. She relived it every night in her dreams. It didn't make it any better that Romero still called her cell phone from time to time, acting as if what he did wasn't that serious.

The two girls sat in the living room talking.

"I'm a nervous wreck, Crea. I answered the phone at least five times today and asked him to stop calling, but he won't. He even had the nerve to apologize and ask if we could start over."

Fiona rested her head in her hands and cried. "I keep replaying that day over and over in my head."

"I'm so sorry, Fi. I can't even imagine . . ." Crea rubbed Fiona's back.

"You know, I partly blame myself for getting in his bed and letting him touch me there. I shouldn't have gone that far. I *knew* I wasn't ready for sex. I guess I was teasing him because I knew I wasn't going to go through with it. And he just forced me. Didn't even care that I was fighting, crying, and screaming."

"You told him no and no means no. Period. I don't care where he touched you. You have the right to change your mind."

"Not with Romero," Fiona said, wiping away the tears that fell from her eyes.

"Fi, we need to go out for a walk—to the mall, the park, anywhere. You name it." Today, Crea wanted to get Fiona out of the house to get her mind off things. The weather was about seventy degrees with no rain in sight.

"That actually sounds like a great idea, Crea, but I'm not in the mood. I just want to stay in bed and watch TV. How about tomorrow?"

"Okay, but I'm holding you to that." Crea gave her a tight hug. "Please change your cell number so that jerk can't call you anymore. I'll see you later," Crea said, heading toward the apartment door.

The following day Fiona called Crea. "Hey, Crea," Fiona said.

"Hey FiFi, I'm getting ready to leave out now."

Fiona sighed. "I don't think I'm up to it today. Can we do it next weekend?" She sounded so depressed.

"Every time we plan something, you back out. I think it would be good for you to get some fresh air. Don't let Romero do this to you. Don't let him control your life. I can't say I understand how it feels to have been raped because I . . ." Crea heard someone outside her bedroom door. "Hold on, Fi." She opened her door, peeked out, and noticed Vince closing his bedroom door. "I'm on my way." She hung up the phone.

When Crea arrived, Fiona answered the door still in her pink and gray striped pajama pants and matching tank top. Crea groaned when she saw her. She knew Fiona wouldn't be leaving the house today.

"Are you sure you don't want to get out for a little while?"

"I'm kind of tired. I didn't get much sleep last night. Next week, okay?" Fiona knew Crea meant well, but lately she just wanted to be alone. She didn't know how to explain it to Crea without hurting her feelings. She didn't feel like being cheered up. However, she appreciated Crea for being there.

"Okay. Well, I brought us a few movies to watch. I brought your favorite, *Love & Basketball* and my favorite, *Madea's Family Reunion*. Plus, three other blockbusters. We don't have to go out to have fun." Crea smiled.

"Thanks for understanding. I haven't been feeling good lately. Every time I think about what happened my stomach turns."

"Maybe you need to see a doctor or a counselor," Crea suggested. "You know I'll go with you."

"Nah, that'll just make things worse. They might start asking questions."

"Well, they may be able to give you something to help you sleep. You won't know if you don't go and check it out."

"Yeah . . . maybe I do need to go. I can hardly stay awake in my classes and I'm always so tired." Fiona brushed her wild mane into a ponytail.

"We can go to the free clinic tomorrow. You don't need an appointment."

"I don't know if I really want to go, though," Fiona said, keeping her thoughts of Romero possibly giving her a disease to herself.

"You have to," Crea said. "We've gotta make sure you're all right. Think about it carefully, Fi. Please," she begged, hoping Fiona would agree to get some help.

Fiona sighed. "Can we watch the movies so I can get this off my mind right now? I don't feel like thinking about this."

"Yeah, I understand," Crea said, walking Fiona toward the living room where the large flat screen TV hung on the wall. "I'm ready to get my laugh on anyway."

They spent the afternoon watching a marathon of their favorite movies. They memorized several lines and recited them right along with Sanaa Lathan and Omar Epps in *Love & Basketball.* They laughed until they cried at Tyler Perry dressed as the gun-toting Madea. Crea was glad to see the old Fiona, even if it was just for a short period of time.

The next day, Crea and Fiona cut school to go to the clinic. It opened at eight and they wanted to get there early to avoid a long wait. Fifteen minutes after she was called back to the examination room, a short female doctor walked into the room and introduced herself as Dr. Singh. She talked to Fiona about her symptoms and later ran a blood and urine sample to the lab.

Two hours later, Dr. Singh returned and allowed Crea into the room after Fiona asked if she could keep her company. "Okay, Fiona, there's not much I can recommend to help you sleep. Sometimes if you take a relaxing bath and drink some tea before going to bed, it will help," the doctor said. "I'm also prescribing you prenatal vitamins. You need to take one every day."

Fiona and Crea looked at each other in shock. The rape was so traumatic they never even considered that Fiona could be pregnant.

After reading the expressions on their faces the doctor said, "I assume you didn't know you are pregnant."

"No, she didn't," Crea spoke for her.

"Well, I need to know where I can go to take care of this." Tears raced down Fiona's cheeks.

Dr. Singh stood next to Fiona and gently touched her shoulder.

Fiona flinched.

Instantly, the doctor removed her hand. "Slow down, okay? This is a very serious decision you're making about something you found out two minutes ago. You need to think about it first and *then* call me in five days. If you still want the information, I'll give it to you."

"There is no *way* I'm keeping this baby, so you may as well give me the address now!" Fiona shouted.

Dr. Singh was surprised at Fiona's reaction. "Give it a little time. Everything will work out. It'll be okay." She gently patted Fiona's arm.

"Yeah? If you call being raped by your boyfriend okay, then I'm okay."

"Sweetie, someone raped you? Did you report it to the police?"

"No, I'm fine. Just please, give me the information so I can get an abortion," Fiona pleaded as she hopped off the exam table.

Dr. Singh looked at Fiona with a serious expression. "You really need to report this to the police. As a physician, I'm obligated to report this. I can call them now if . . ."

Fiona quickly nodded her head no several times. "No! You don't understand. I can't—I'll only deny it and I won't press any charges."

"Listen, sweetheart, being raped is psychologically de—"

"Raped? Who mentioned anything about a rape? I know I didn't," Fiona said, pointing at herself then glancing at Crea.

The doctor held her hands out in surrender. "Okay, okay then. I think you need to talk to a friend of mine. Please. She's a counselor. Maybe she can help you sort out your emotions before you make any decisions. I can call her right now so we can set up an appointment."

"I think that's a great idea, Fiona. I'll go with you," Crea encouraged as she grabbed Fiona's hand.

"No. My mind is already made up. I don't want a baby," Fiona stated firmly.

"Fi, please. Just hear the doctor out first, then you can do what you think is best. Please? For me?" Crea begged.

"Okay, I'll talk to her, but I doubt if I'll change my mind."

"That's all I ask," Dr. Singh said. "Rape victims go through a lot of emotional stress, which can lead to depression and other illnesses. I just want you to talk to Dr. Tyler and go from there. That's all."

"Okay, I'll talk to her," Fiona said, although she didn't sound convincing.

"Good. Wait here please. I'll call her up for you." The doctor paused, looking sympathetically at Fiona. "Sweetie, I'm so sorry, but I'll still have to report the rape. I'm really sorry."

"Do what you gotta do, 'cause I am," Fiona said, crossing her arms and staring at the ceiling.

"Please don't leave. I'll get the doctor." Dr. Singh said as she rushed out of the room.

Crea hugged Fiona tight. There were no words she could think of to comfort her. They stood in the middle of the floor and cried together.

"How could this be happening to me?" Fiona wailed.

NINETY-NINE PROBLEMS

CHAPTER 14

Waiting made them anxious. Vincent and Marcus sat on the bleachers at Garfield Park waiting their turn to play a game of three-on-three basketball. Marcus was now fully recovered. The fact that it was ninety degrees in the shade didn't deter them from coming out to play. It was three in the afternoon and the outdoor pool and playground areas were packed with laughing children. A Little League baseball game was in progress on the other side of the park.

Vince's cell phone vibrated in his pocket. He pulled it out and the caller-ID read private caller. "Hello?" he answered.

"Oh, I have to call you private in order for you to answer the phone? What's up with that?" the female voice asked.

"Who is this?" Vince answered with a frown.

"Vince, don't play with me, boy. You know who this is. Why haven't you called me?" Tameka asked, smacking her lips.

"Girl, what you want? You got the nerve to burn me, then ask why I haven't called you? Be real."

"What? I didn't burn you. I don't have nothin'. Besides, you were the first guy I have ever slept with."

"Ha ha ha. You expect me to believe that? I know when a female has been around and you have definitely been around. So, I'm gonna need you to lose this number. It's a rap for you, shorty," Vince said coldly.

"What? Whateva! You wasn't all that good anyway," Tameka yelled. "I've had way better," she said before hanging up.

Vince glanced at Marcus. "I can't believe this trick! She's calling, acting like she's innocent. Then gon' lie and say she ain't never been with nobody but me. Then when I tell her she's cut off, she claims she's had better. Man, that female is crazy!" Vince said shaking his head.

"Straight up? She said that? That's hilarious." Marcus laughed. "Almost as ridiculous as this cake I'm about to make. This drop gon' set my pockets straight for a minute."

Vince's brows drew in as he frowned. "You doing weight already, man? If you get busted, you'll be locked down for a minute. You know that, right? If that happens, you won't be making *no* money. Feel me?"

"I told you, I ain't tryna be out here on corners for long. I'm tryna do big things so I can make some real money. I got a shorty to take care of. Crazy Mike is taking me with him to show me how it's done. We meetin' up with Romero and his crew tonight behind those old steel mills. Romero got connections with this big time Dominican. I'm making five G's for just going."

"Romero?" Vince tapped Marcus on the arm. "Ol' boy who used to go to Fenton?"

"Yeah, that stud," Marcus said, glancing across the street at a crowd of guys that didn't look familiar. "I'll be right back. I see Crazy Mike coming up the block. Let me go holler at him real quick. Keep your eyes peeled for them dudes right there, though, V." Marcus swept his eyes over at the circle of guys to make Vince aware. "They on somethin'."

Marcus jumped off the bleachers and jogged away.

"Hurry up, man. We up next," Vincent shouted as Marcus left.

A familiar car approached the park and settled into a parking space. Vince shook his head as soon as he spotted Mr. Mercer walking toward him. *What is he doing up here? Following me?*

"What's up, Mercer?" Vince asked, meeting him halfway.

"Oh, not much. How you doing?" Mr. Mercer extended his hand for a shake.

"I'm good," Vince answered as he gripped his hand. "What're you doing around here?" Vince kneeled to tie his shoes.

"Not much, I was on my way to your house to talk to your mom. She had a few pictures of your dad she wanted me to have." He glanced around the park. "So how's school coming along? One more year and it's college time for you."

"It's cool," Vince said, smiling as he thought about being away on his own.

"Did I just see a smile? That's a first. You have to get the grades to get into a good college or university. Think about what you're interested in doing, then research it. You have one year left, man. Now's the time to at least start planning out the rest of your life."

"A year is a long time, Mercer," Vince said, looking back at the court to see if his turn was coming up.

"I used to think so, too, but what a difference a day makes, man." Vince immediately knew he was talking about his father's death. He could feel that old anger starting to rise.

"Yeah, okay."

Mr. Mercer mocked Vince and stared him down. "Life is short, McCloud." He placed his huge hands in his pockets and rocked on his feet. "I want you to live a long and peaceful life, young blood. Your mom does too, so get serious about it. I'm not saying don't be a teenager; I'm saying consider what's out there waiting for you—an education, a trade school, or jail and death. Make a wise choice, Vince. You can't goof your way through school and think you'll land solidly on your feet. Consequences come with everything." He glanced across the street. "And be careful out here, too. Those cats over there look like they're up to no good. I'll see you around. You should probably head home."

"Aw, they ain't on nothin'." Vince waved his hand. "This Dragon territory. Crazy Mike got this on lock. I'ma go home after I run this court a couple of times. Show these amateurs how it's done," Vince said, looking away from him and over at the same guys Marcus had also warned him about. *At least I hope these dudes ain't on nothing.* "And thanks, Mercer. I heard you. All of it."

Mr. Mercer nodded. "If you ever need to talk, you know where to find me."

"I just might do that," Vince said. They shook hands and Vince walked back toward the court. Mr. Mercer got in his car, giving the small huddle of guys a final glance before driving off.

Twenty minutes later, it was time for them to play, but Marcus wasn't back yet. Vince and two other guys from his neighborhood teamed up to play the winning team.

Ten minutes into the game Vince dribbled the ball between his legs, ran to the opposite end of the court, leaped in the air and slammed the ball through the net. As his feet hit the asphalt, gunfire rang out across the street. Most of the guys on the basketball court ran in the opposite direction while others lay flat on the ground near Vince. Screams and screeching tires echoed in the air. When the gunfire stopped, Vince raised his head and looked toward the commotion.

"Oh, snap! Marcus!" Vincent ran across the street to look for Marcus. A boy wearing all black with a face mask lay motionless on the stairs of Al's Barbershop. Another lay near the curb outside of Oakton's Liquor. Vince's heart beat rapidly while he continued to scan the area. As he turned the corner, Marcus walked out of a two-flat brownstone building.

"What up, V?" Marcus said, breathing hard. "Did you see that, man? Some fools tried to put us to sleep. Did anybody get dropped?" Marcus looked around.

Vince couldn't believe how calm Marcus was reacting. The fact that he had just come so close to being killed didn't bother him one bit. Vince could almost swear he was smirking.

123

"Um, yeah. I saw two down. We need to bounce, Money."

"Wait, let's go see who it is." Vince suddenly froze in place. His brows raised and his eyes grew wide at the masked man coming up behind Marcus with a gun drawn.

"Boom!"

The gunman shot Marcus in the back of the head. His body went limp and instantly hit the ground. Next, he turned the gun on Vince and pulled the trigger three times. When he realized the gun was out of bullets he just stared at Vince. "Today's your lucky day, *big brother*," the gunman said, running toward a blue Chevy Blazer. He hopped in on the passenger's side as the driver sped off, swerving out of control.

Vince wanted to scream, cry, run, anything, but just as he did when his father fell to his death, he froze. His body trembled and his heart felt like it was going to jump right out of his chest. The distant sound of sirens snapped him out of his trance. He looked at Marcus. His left leg was positioned awkwardly under his torso and his eyes were wide open. Vincent pulled his T-shirt over his head and kneeled down next to Marcus. He lifted his head and pressed the garment against the bullet hole, trying to stop the river of blood flowing out of his dome. When the white shirt turned red in mere seconds, Vincent realized there wasn't much hope for his friend. He took one last look in Marcus's eyes and knew he was gone. Vince brushed his hand over Marcus's eyes to shut them as he fought back tears.

"Naw . . . not Marcus, too," Crazy Mike said, walking up from out of nowhere. "Deg, he was my best soldier, the best hustler out here." He shook his head and cursed.

124

You the reason he's dead. Vince wanted to break Crazy Mike's jaw. But he knew he didn't stand a chance against him. "He was my best friend and he didn't deserve to die like this," Vince responded in a forceful tone.

Crazy Mike stood over Vince while glancing down at Marcus's dead body. "Unfortunately, lil' man, this is all part of the game. You live fast, you just might die young. This is the life he chose. He knew what it involved, so don't swell up at me. You were smart enough to fall back, 'cause that could've been you." Crazy Mike shook his head, got in his black Escalade truck and drove off.

Vince's eyes were blurred with tears when the officers stepped out of the car ordering him to stand to his feet.

"On your feet now!" the officer yelled.

"The guys who did this were driving a—" Vince started babbling.

"Shut up and raise your hands above your head!" the officer commanded.

A knot formed in Vince's throat when he realized the officers were the same two that beat him and Marcus. He hoped they didn't recognize him.

Kozlowski patted him down and tightly placed handcuffs on his wrist.

"Why you putting handcuffs on me? I didn't do anything. You're wasting time with me when you could be going after the real killers," Vince argued.

"Tell it to the judge because you're going to jail today, son."

"Wait a minute, I remember you," Officer Jefferson said, pointing at Vince.

He turned and looked down at Marcus's corpse. "Umm, I see Mr. Tough Guy wasn't so tough after all." Both men laughed simultaneously.

"That ain't funny, man," Vincent shouted. "My friend is lying there dead and y'all crackin' jokes."

Jefferson grabbed him by the forearm and shoved him in back of the squad car. "Don't worry about him. He'll be dust pretty soon. You better worry about spending twenty years in jail for his murder."

The officers had been questioning him about the shooting for the last five hours. Vince was tired, cold, and hungry. The officers weren't listening to anything he had to say, so he stopped talking about an hour ago. They kept trying to get him to confess to Marcus's murder, but there was no way Vince would write any such statement. They had left the room twenty minutes ago. Vince used the time to rest his head on the table in front of him. This all felt like a bad dream. He couldn't believe Marcus was dead. He couldn't believe how close he had come to death. Quickly, Vince lifted his head when he heard the door opening.

"Now that you've had some rest, can you tell us what really happened out there? Did he cheat you out of your cut of the drug money and you got mad and shot him? If you tell us the truth now, the judge may take it easy on you." Kozlowski tried to make Vince believe he was trying to help him, but Vince knew better. The good cop/bad cop routine had been done to death.

"Come on, son. Tell us where the gun is." Jefferson leaned closer to Vince.

The door flew open and in walked three men. Vince felt like a weight was lifted off his chest when he saw Mr. Mercer among them. The gentleman in the white shirt was referred to as Captain Leak.

"My name is Daniel Brody, Mr. McCloud's attorney," the tall, balding man declared. As your captain here will confirm, you have no grounds to keep Vincent here any longer." He placed a business card on the table. "If you have any further questions for my client in the future, I will need to be present."

Officer Kozlowski removed the cuffs from Vince's wrists. Vince rubbed each wrist in an attempt to relieve the pain.

"Come on, Vince, let's get you home," Mr. Mercer said.

Vince walked up to him, hugged him tight, and cried profusely. He now knew that using his one phone call to contact Mr. Mercer was the right thing to do.

NINETY-NINE PROBLEMS

CHAPTER 15

Fresh gear, fresh ride, fresh chick on my side....dudes jockin', Glock cockin', money rockin' my pockets," Marcus flowed while bobbing his head.

"Wooo, okay. That's tight. Sounds like my skills are rubbing off on you," Vince teased.

"Man, please. My flow always been sick. In fact, I'm thinking about trying out for 106 & Park Freestyle Friday."

Vince bent over in laughter. He nearly fell off the bleachers they were sitting on in the park. "Marcus, man, I can't let you go out like that. I can't let you go on TV and embarrass yourself in front of millions."

Marcus pulled his dreads back off his face. "Ha ha, there you go, Mr. Funny Man. Always got jokes. Let's hear what you got!" Marcus challenged.

"You sure you want some of this?" Vince got up and started rocking to the beat in his head. He froze mid-sentence when he saw a hooded man run up behind Marcus, put a gun to his head and pull the trigger in what seemed like two seconds. Vince suddenly sprang up from his pillow in a cold sweat.

Marcus's funeral was so packed with students and faculty from Fenton Fractional High School that some attendees had to stand against the walls. Marcus's mother took it the hardest. Family members had to pull her away from the casket. Vince wondered if she felt guilty for letting her drug addiction come in between her relationship with her son. He also wondered how Marcus's son would turn out without his father being around.

Seeing Principal Williams choke back tears during the service made him angry. After all the bad things she'd said about Marcus, she had the nerve to shed tears. She even gave Marcus's mother a tight hug. Vince just shook his head. He had already passed the casket and expressed condolences to his friend's family. Vince walked toward the exit.

Mr. Mercer stood way in the back of the room near the exit. When Vince walked out, he followed behind him.

"Vince, you okay, man?"

"Naw, not really. I just need to get outta here," Vince shook his head as he fought back tears.

"You wanna go somewhere and talk?"

"I do need to talk but not now. Can I come by your office on Monday?" Tears were now racing down his face.

"Anytime," Mr. Mercer replied.

Vince quickly wiped the tear away, and then headed to his car. He went home and locked himself in his bedroom. He didn't turn on the television or answer his cell phone. He lay back in his bed and stared up at the ceiling. He eventually dozed off.

Vince and his dad were sitting on the edge of the dock at the lake where his father used to take him fishing. His dad's voice was as clear as a glass of spring water.

"Son, talk to me. What's going on with you? You're getting in trouble at school and your mother is worried sick."

"You're supposed to be here. Mom shouldn't have to raise me alone. I hate you for leaving me! Why did you have to go?" Vince wept uncontrollably.

"Don't you know that if I could turn back time, I'd be there with you, Crea, and your mom? I'd give anything to be a part of your life right now. But the Lord didn't have it in the cards for me, Junior. It was my time to go and we can't undo that. But you hurting your mom is inexcusable. She loves you very much and she doesn't deserve the pain you're causing her." Mr. McCloud lifted Vince's chin and looked him in the eyes. *"You need to get it together, son. I'm sorry that your friend is dead, but you have a second chance to turn things around. You need to take school more seriously; start preparing for your future. You can't stop living because I'm not here. I'll always be with you."*

"Dad, I didn't—"

"And why are you treating these young ladies like doormats? I raised you better than that. You're supposed to respect the girls like you would want someone to respect your sister or mother," Mr. McCloud lectured.

Vince gasped and sat up swiftly as he heard a door close. As much as he tried to shake off the dreams, they kept coming. He knew it was time to make a change. Vince got out of bed and headed to the bathroom down the hall, noticing his mother's bedroom light still on. He gently knocked.

"Come in," his mother responded.

"Hey, Momma."

She closed her Bible and looked at him. "What are you doing up so early? Can't sleep?"

"Naw." He looked down at his feet.

"Are you okay? I know you and Marcus were really close. I'm really sorry about what happened."

Vince shrugged. "I guess I'm okay. I keep having these dreams, so I haven't been getting too much sleep lately." He walked over and sat on the edge of his mother's bed.

"You want to talk about them?" Mrs. McCloud gave Vince her undivided attention.

"Naw, but I do want to apologize for how I've been acting. Marcus's death made me realize that tomorrow ain't promised to anyone. I think Dad's death affected me more than I thought. I've been so mad at him for leaving, but I know now that he'd be here if he could."

Mrs. McCloud nodded as her eyes welled with tears.

"I haven't been doing my best in school, hanging out with the wrong dudes, and playing girls, knowing that Dad taught me better. I think I'm just mad and felt like I was getting back at Dad, but now I know that it's only hurting me." He looked down at the carpeted floor.

Mrs. McCloud eased over and embraced her son. "Your dad loved you and Crea so much. Don't ever forget that. His family came before everything."

"Yeah, I know, Ma. I'm sorry for hurting you."

132

"Aww, baby, it's okay. Just promise that you'll come talk to me next time and not just shut me out," she said, pulling back and looking him in the eyes.

"I promise. I got a lot of stuff I need to get out, so you ready?" Vince asked.

"I'm all ears," Kathy replied.

Vince began at his father's death and even revealed his STD scare. She warned Vince about condoms, but preferred he not have sex at all. Vince felt awkward at first, but after opening up to his mother about his feelings, he felt like he'd been given new air to breathe. It was like a heavy weight had been taken off his shoulders. Right when they ended their conversation, Vince told his mom, "I'ma holler at Mercer, too. He knows a lot and he's a pretty cool dude."

"Your father always chose his friends wisely," she said. "You should do the same. Make sure you have positive things in common with the people you let into your life."

"I hear you, Ma." Vince kissed her on the cheek, then went to lay back down while his mother finished getting ready for work.

NINETY-NINE PROBLEMS

CHAPTER 16

C rea kneeled down to pray. *Lord, I didn't get any sleep last night. I'm so worried about Fiona getting this abortion today. She won't even consider any other options. I don't agree with her decision, but I guess I can understand why she would want to go through with it. The baby would probably be a constant reminder of the rape. But I just feel the baby is innocent in all this and shouldn't have to suffer. Lord, maybe you can help her find it in her heart to change her mind.*

She stood to her feet, wiped her tear-stained face, and then headed to the bathroom to get ready.

The rain violently beat against Vince's windshield as he sat outside Fiona's apartment building. She had asked him to drive her to the clinic.

"Vince, thanks for giving me a ride. Where's Crea?" Fiona asked as she opened the door and sat in the passenger seat while letting down her umbrella.

"She wasn't ready, so I left her. I woke her up in enough time," Vince said. "I didn't want you to be late."

"Thanks." Fiona's shoulders rose as she deeply exhaled her disappointment at her best friend's absence. Crea knew how nervous she was about this whole thing. "Well, I appreciate you not asking me any questions or judging me about being pregnant or for what I'm about to do. I know some people say it's wrong, but I just can't keep this baby." Tears slid down Fiona's cheeks as she spoke. "You don't have to hang around. I can call you when I'm finished," she said as Vince pulled in front of the clinic.

"Don't I always have your back? You have to do what you have to do for you. Who am I to tell you what choices to make with your life?" He looked in her eyes without blinking. "Go on in and I'll be in when I find a parking spot."

Fiona's legs quivered as she walked in the door of the one-story building. It was eight in the morning and the waiting area was half-full with mostly young girls. She checked in at the reception desk. A Hispanic woman with heavy eyeliner and dark lipstick handed her three forms to fill out and told her to have a seat. Fiona kept her eyes focused on the paperwork as she walked back to the waiting area and sat down.

Vince entered the clinic and took a seat next to her as she filled out the forms.

"Are you okay?" Vince whispered, placing his hand on her arm. "You're shaking."

Fiona looked Vince in his eyes and said softly, "I'm scared, but the thought of keeping this baby scares me even more. I don't know what I'd do without you and Crea."

"I know I mess with you all the time, but you know I got your back?"

"I know, and thanks again for loaning me half the money. I'm going to get a job and pay you back as soon as I can."

Thirty minutes had passed before a gray-haired woman called Fiona to the back. Vince didn't know what to say, so he kept silent as she got up and disappeared through the door.

Sitting in the clinic made him think about the possibility of getting Tameka or one of his other girls pregnant. He knew he had to stop all the sleeping around. He had already gotten burned once, and he definitely wasn't ready for a baby, or worse, HIV or AIDS.

Fiona returned to the waiting area two hours later. She glanced around the room and spotted Crea sitting next to Vince, who was knocked out in the same seat he was in when she left. His head rested against the wall as he slept with his mouth partially open.

Crea got up, walked toward Fiona, and hugged her.

"I thought you faked me out," Fiona's voice quivered as she spoke.

"Fi, you know I would never leave you hanging. All I had to do was throw on my clothes. Vince's stupid butt knew he could've waited five more minutes. I had to catch two buses to get here," Crea said, rolling her eyes at her brother.

"I'm just glad you're here," Fiona said.

Vince awoke and looked around with one eyebrow raised, not recalling that he was at the clinic. He sat on the edge of his seat and wiped saliva from the corner of his mouth. "You ready to go home?" He stood up and pulled his car keys out of his pocket.

"Yeah, let's get outta here," Fiona answered.

137

"Are you okay?" Crea asked.

Fiona shrugged. "I guess."

The walk back to the car was silent. Fiona finally shook her head and said, "I couldn't do it. I couldn't kill this baby. Sorry I wasted your time." Her voice quaked as she fought back tears. "Here's your money, too." She placed the folded bills in Vince's hand.

Thank you God, Crea thought.

They got in the car and Vince pulled off. Fiona looked out the window before finally speaking. "He . . ." She paused to think about her next words. "Romero . . . raped me." She cried softly.

"I know," Vince said sympathetically. He placed his hand on her shoulder to comfort her.

Fiona turned around and looked at Crea, who was sitting in the back seat. "Crea told you? She wasn't supposed to tell anyone."

"I didn't tell him anything!" Crea said. "You know me better than that."

"Naw, she didn't tell me," Vince said. "I overheard her talking to you on the phone a couple of times. Don't worry, Fi. I would never tell anyone. I understand why you wanted to have the abortion, so I'm not judging you." He softly touched her hand.

"I don't know what I'm going to do, but I know I have to tell my mother soon. I wish I would have listened to you when you tried to warn me about Romero. I didn't want to hear it and now look at me." She wiped tears from her face. "I heard he got locked up—a drug bust or something. I guess God really don't like ugly."

"I know I won't shed any tears if he's locked up," Crea commented and poked out her lips.

"Yeah, he got arrested the same night Marcus was killed. The police rolled up on them during a drug deal behind the old steel mill. I heard there was a shoot-out and a couple of dudes got killed. Romero and three other guys got arrested and Crazy Mike was the only one that got away. I'm sure Romero will be on lock for a long time with the amount of drugs involved in that bust. Lil' Reese from around the way just got out of the county jail the other day. He said Romero's booty got jacked in the shower."

"Really? Well, now he knows how I feel," Fiona said. "I hope he gets everything he deserves in there."

"Don't worry, he will," Vince assured.

He was glad he'd made that anonymous call to the police that night. Marcus had given him all the details and he passed it on to the police. Romero had raped Fiona and killed Marcus and there was no way he was going to let the whole "no snitch" rule stop him. It was too bad Crazy Mike got away. He replaced Marcus the next day and had the new guy selling drugs on the same corner where Marcus's blood still stained the pavement.

Crea looked out the window toward the sky. *Dad, things seem a little upside down right now, but I think we're going to be okay.*

Vince pressed the play button on his CD, turned up the volume and nodded his head to Jay-Z's single "99 Problems" as they rode the rest of the way home in silence.

Ninety-Nine Problems

Discussion Questions

1. Do you think Fiona's attraction to bad boys got her what she deserved?

2. Should Crea have told Brandon how she felt sooner or do you agree she made the right choice by waiting on him to reveal his feelings first?

3. Do you think Principal Williams was wrong in how she handled Vincent and his friend Marcus? If so, how do you think she should've handled it?

4. Why do you think Vince chose not to sell drugs?

5. How do you feel about Fiona choosing Romeo over Crea? Do you think Crea should have just minded her own business regarding their relationship and been there for Fiona no matter what?

6. Fiona was accepting money and other things from Romero. Should she have expected him to want something from her in return?

7. Do you think Vince deserved to end up with a sexually transmitted disease for sleeping around with different girls, unprotected?

8. In the end, Romero got what he deserved. Would you have made that anonymous call to the police like Vince or do you consider that snitching?

9. How do you feel about Fiona's decision regarding the abortion?

10. What character do you most relate to and why?

11. Crea and Vince lost their father early. How important is a dad's presence in the household and did they all suffer from his absence?

WAHIDA CLARK PRESENTS

Y.A.
YOUNG ADULT

THE BOY IS MINE!

A WILSON HIGH CONFIDENTIAL

A YOUNG ADULT NOVEL BY

CHARMAINE WHITE

NEISHA

"Girl, why did we sign up for study hall?" Neisha's friend, Bryanna asked while looking around the small classroom. It was the first day of the new term, and Bryanna had no clue why she let Neisha pick out her schedule.

"Because, you know we need some time to get all this homework off of our backs," Neisha replied, happy with her quick response, but to her displeasure, Bryanna saw right through it.

"Why are you trying to front me off? I'm not stupid, girl; I know the only reason you *really* signed up for this dumb class was to get another peak at Marcus Hamilton," she said, looking her close friend up and down. "You're not slick, girl; I can see right through you."

"Whatever, Bre, I am not thinking about him; he's not even that cute." Now this time she had to smile because everybody knows how fine Marcus is. Six-foot tall, medium-brown complexion, with the darkest, most mesmerizing eyes Neisha has ever seen. No lie. Every girl wants him. Who wouldn't? He's in the most popular group at school, very attractive, and it's more than easy to crush on him.

"Once again, you're playing yourself if you really think I'm gonna fall for that. I saw you staring him down in Civics last hour, and um, I kinda saw him checking you out right back," Bryanna said, looking at Neisha for any sign of excitement.

"What! He was looking at me? When? Bryanna, don't play like this!" Neisha watched Bryanna to see if she was joking around. Bryanna looked serious enough, and Neisha couldn't help but get excited. "How do you know he was looking at me? He could've been looking at someone else. You know how he's always checking out somebody, looking for the next girl to hook up with." Neisha grabbed Bryanna by her shoulders, staring in her face, with her eyebrows raised high, and a huge smile plastered upon her pretty face.

Bryanna put on a sneaky grin. "I knew you liked him! Girl, I was just playin' with you. If he was looking at you, I surely didn't notice. Oh! I got you good with this one! There's no way you can try to get out of that. Damn girl, he's got you sprung. If you could only see the way your face lit up when I told you. Now *that* one was priceless!"

"Bre! That was not funny. I can't believe I fell for that weak story. You really just pissed me off," she said, looking around for a place to sit in the back of the classroom. Even though she was mad, she couldn't help but add, "And just because I got

excited, doesn't mean I like him or anything. If I liked him, I would've made him my man by now."

Neisha knew this was true. In her mind, she was all that with her long brown hair, smooth, light brown skin, and a body that most girls work their entire lives trying to pull off. Not to mention she's co-captain of the cheerleading team. Everyone knows that when Neisha's around, they had better hope their boyfriend isn't checking her out.

Bryanna stopped smiling. "Just because you're cute doesn't mean you're Marcus's type," she said.

"What's that supposed to mean?" Neisha asked, slightly offended.

"You know what I mean," she said, finally taking a seat at the desk way in the back of the classroom. Neisha followed suit. "Marcus is a Clique Boy," she concluded, as if that was the end of the discussion, but Neisha didn't seem to be catching on.

"*And?*" Neisha asked, looking at her friend as if what she said made no sense at all.

Bryanna replied in an exasperated tone, "It means, girl that when you're a Clique Boy, you're a player, and when you're a player at Wilson, you don't really treat girls with much respect. You must not have heard what happened with Marcus and Trish, huh?" She hoped she made her point clear enough that Neisha needed to back off Marcus, if she knew what was good for her.

"What happened was Trish's own fault. It doesn't mean I'm gonna do what she did, not saying that I'd ever hookup with Marcus. Like I said before, I don't want him; he's not my type."

Neisha didn't really care about what happened between Marcus and some freshman. More kids began arriving in the classroom.

"Well then, what exactly is your type? Because last I checked, you had a *thing* for Wilson High's Bad Boy," Bryanna said with a smirk on her face. "Tell the truth. If you like the boy, I'm not gonna knock your game or anything."

This time Neisha let out a loud snort that caught some of the students' attention. She whispered, "Knock *my* game? How could you ever knock my game? Girl, I'm the shiznit—the queen up in here. Bryanna, you are seriously trippin'. Like I said before, I don't want that boy."

"Oh really?" Bryanna said, folding her arms and giving one of her charming, yet devilish smirks.

"Yeah really," Neisha replied, folding her arms just like Bryanna. She looked across the room, trying hard to play it off, but once again, Bryanna caught her in the act.

"There's your little boyfriend," she said, moving her eyes in the direction of the sexy, confident boy walking into the room with one of his friends.

Neisha replied in a strong but silent whisper, "He's *not* my boyfriend, and if you say that again I'm gonna—"

"What? Make up a cheer about me? Neisha, we all know that you are not the violent type, so don't even try to front like you are," Bryanna said, slightly mocking her. "By the way, where is the teacher for this class? It seems like we've been waiting in here for an hour. I mean, the bell hasn't rung or anything,"

Neisha stared at a very pretty girl walking in just as the last bell rang. The girl was tall and thick, just the way the boys like

them, with light hazel eyes and curly black hair that seemed to go on forever. She was followed into the room by an old man who seemed to be obsessed with her butt.

"Take a seat, Ms. Andrews, right over there by those two ladies," Mr. Polk, the study hall teacher said, pointing in the direction of Neisha and Bryanna.

"Why I gotta sit way in the back?" Lynda asked with an attitude.

Mr. Polk replied tiredly, "Because I'm the teacher, and whatever I say, goes."

Then Lynda replied, "Oh is that right?"

"Yes, Lynda, that's right. Now go take a seat before I give you a detention. *Now,*" Mr. Polk added. *I can"t stand teaching ghetto students like you, he thought.*

Lynda obviously didn't care what Mr. Polk said, for she said loud enough for everyone to hear, "Detention my behind," and everyone in the class started laughing.

"And what a beautiful behind it is," Marcus commented. Lynda made her way to the back of the class, making sure she lingered near Marcus while passing the row. Lynda gave Marcus a flirty look. "What did you say to me?" she asked.

"You heard me," Marcus said in a low tone, but loud enough for even Neisha and Bryanna to hear. "I said you have a beautiful behind." Marcus's boys gave him a dap. But Neisha didn't find it too amusing.

"Did you hear what he just said to her?" she asked Bryanna, pissed off.

"Why do you care? I thought you said you didn't like him," Bryanna said in a matter-of-fact voice.

5

"I don't, but that's still some bogus stuff to say to a girl," said Neisha, still trying to eavesdrop on Marcus and Lynda's conversation.

Lynda replied to Marcus in her one-of-a-kind, ghetto voice,

"You can say whatever you want about my behind, but it still won't belong to you."

"Not for long." Marcus answered, giving her one of his signature, sexy looks.

"Oh really?" Lynda said, cocking her head to the side.

Marcus winked. "It's all up to you," he whispered so that even Neisha couldn't hear.

Lynda grinned and made her way to the back of the classroom, sitting right next to Neisha. Marcus stared directly at her butt the entire time. Eventually his gaze fell straight onto Neisha, giving her a once-over look. With all her might, Neisha couldn't stop staring at the boy! He was looking so good. She just couldn't keep her eyes off him.

Marcus noticed her checking him out, so he gave her another once-over. He turned back to his boys, tapped Drew on the arm, and then whispered something to him. Drew looked back in Neisha's direction, who quickly averted her eyes. They both gave each other a fist pound after Drew whispered something to Marcus.

"Damn girl, why do they keep on lookin' back here?" Bryanna said in Neisha's ear.

"Bryanna, I messed up! Shoot, I was staring at him, and I was staring *hard*. I don't know why, but I just couldn't help myself. Marcus noticed, and then I guess he told his boys to look back here and check me out or something because that's all

they've been doing for the last five minutes. *Damn*! I don't know what came over me. This is so embarrassing. What if they're saying something about me? You *know* how fast rumors get spread around Wilson!" Neisha was so upset by her spur of the moment fixation of Marcus, she didn't even notice the boy in front of her was trying to hand her a note.

"*Psst,* Neisha, pay attention. Here, Drew told me to give this to you," this boy, Sam said, looking curiously at the note.

Before Neisha could take the note, Bryanna took it and read it first.

Neisha wanted to hurry and take the note from Bryanna, but she didn't want to cause a scene in front of the class, so she just waited it out until Bryanna was done reading it.

Hold up. Drew? The same Drew sitting next to the boy I'm crushing on? The same boy who's friends with the boy who just caught me staring at him? This could not be happening to me!

Oh, but it was, and Bryanna gave her all the proof she needed when she was done reading the note.

Bryanna had a look of pure disbelief on her face. "Here girl, you have to read this for yourself," she said.

Neisha gave Bryanna a cautious look, like she was too nervous to even take the note from her hand, "What is it? What in the world could Drew possibly want that would make you look at me that way?"

"You're gonna have to look for yourself," Bryanna said, passesing the note to Neisha. She tried to give all her attention to Mr. Polk, who seemed to be boring the hell out of everyone in the room. Neisha heard a faint, "I can't believe this," out of

Bryanna's mouth, but tried to ignore it. Whatever this note said had to be something major to get under Bryanna's skin.

She couldn't wait to find out what it was.

MARCUS

Wednesday, 10:00 A.M.
ON THE WAY TO STUDY HALL

"What's up, Torean?" Marcus called to his friend, who was making his way down the hall with some fine chick on his side.

"Nothin' much, just gettin' my game up," Torean replied, nodding his head in the direction of the girl who seemed to be glued to his hip.

"I got you," Marcus said, giving his boy dap, "You know, man, I'm tryna get my game up, too, but these females at Wilson startin' to lose their luster."

"Negro, please. It's not the ladies losin' their luster," Torean said, looking at his friend like he was crazy or something. "It's your behind that can't seem to keep a girl for more than a day."

At this, Marcus had to chortle. Everybody around school knew the deal with Marcus and his crew. When you're a Clique Boy, you had to make sure you switched your girl up from time to time, but Marcus switched his up just about every day of the

9

week. He thought of himself as a "major player," meaning he couldn't let the girls think they owned him or anything.

"Man, don't hate, Torean, just because your ugly self can't help but keep your women for more than two days, doesn't mean my game is on empty," Marcus said with that same trace of laughter in his voice.

Torean cocked his head and gave a big smile. "Me, ugly? Now Marcus, you are seriously off if you think that mess is true. I'm like the finest guy at this school, so don't even front my life off like that," he said. "And everyone, I mean *everyone;* boys and girls alike, know that I am." Torean is the leader of the Clique Boys. Tall, caramel complexion, and super sexy. Everybody and their momma wanted the chance to holler at him. Torean could get anyone he wanted, and if he didn't want you that meant you're a nobody.

Since Marcus is Torean's best friend, he decided to let that little comment go, but he added, "You need to be tryna get at a chick that's gonna give you something that will make you wanna stick around with her for more than a day, man. I've been hearing around school that plenty of females ain't feelin' you no more. So you better get your game up, or that 'Clique Boy' title you struttin' around with gonna be gone in a quick second."

"Man, hell naw. I still get girls. You see Lynda's still on my jock, tryna get at me. But I'm really not tryna get at that; I want a classy chick this time around," Marcus said while his friends gathered around. Torean even seemed to brush off the girl connected to his hip.

"So what are you saying? You want a classy chick? *What?* Did one of those tricks give you something, and now you tryna change your ways? I know you ain't goin' out like that!" Marcus's friend, Drew, also a member of the Clique Boys, asked him. Everyone started to laugh and gave Drew his props for coming up with the joke.

Once the noise quieted, Marcus answered, "No, it's not even like that. I just wanna get with a female who doesn't act like a straight up fool every time I'm ready to drop them, like Trish did. That girl was out of her mind when I told her I was done with her. I'm not tryna have any more females actin' like that around me."

"I told you not to be messin' with those freshmen, no matter how easy they may be," Torean told Marcus, reminiscing on that day Trish called herself causing a scene by cursing Marcus out recklessly in front of everyone when Marcus kicked her off to the side.

Marcus ignored his friend's comment, and turned toward the hallway, suddenly pausing. The girl he kept his eye on was walking down the hall with one of her friends. Since his freshmen year at Wilson High School, he has secretly wanted her, but she was way too stuck up and full of herself for his liking. When he first saw her today in his Civics class, he didn't get a chance to check her out the way he wanted to. She sat way in the back, whereas he preferred to be right in the center of everything. So while she strutted down the hall with her girl, he couldn't help but let his eyes linger on her. *Damn, she is fine.* This was the classy girl he needed to bring his player's status all the way up.

Drew and Torean caught him watching her. Drew asked, "Aye, what are you checkin' out Neisha and her girl for? We all know those stuck up girls are off limits."

"Yeah, I know, but *Damn*. I mean *Damn*, she looks good. I know I can get at that if I step my game up, man. Everybody wants this." He pointed to himself. "So why think that she ain't feelin ya boy, too?" Marcus said cockily.

"Well, if she does holler at you, that means she got off that high pedestal she was on last year when she thought no guy was good enough to holler at her conceited self. Boy, if you can get at that, you gotta be working with somethin' that none of us got," Torean said, looking around at his boys for some sign of agreement.

Drew looked up at the clock. 10:15 A.M. He tapped Marcus. "Hey, don't we have to be at that study hall class at 10:20?" he asked.

"Oh yeah, I forgot about that. A'ight, man, let's be out of here before Polk starts trippin'," Marcus said to Drew. Both of them said bye to their crew and made their way down the hall to the classroom.

The only reason they were taking this class was because they didn't have to do anything in there, but mostly because Marcus overheard Neisha's friend, Bryanna saying how pissed she was that Neisha signed them both up for study hall. Marcus knew they were headed there when he saw them a minute ago, but he tried to play it off. He wouldn't dare tell any of his boys this, but he was definitely looking forward to his next class.

When he reached the door, he heard Bryanna's loudmouth voice saying something about him, but he wasn't sure what it

was, so he ignored it. People were always talking about him, so he wasn't all that surprised.

As he entered the room, he saw Neisha sitting there. He could've sworn she was looking directly at him, but before he could double check this fact, she shifted her gaze in another direction.

Marcus and Drew sat by their boy, Louis near the corner of the room. Just as he was getting settled in his seat, in walked Lynda. Marcus was feeling the girl and all; she did have a banging body, but she was just too ghetto for his taste. Lynda's eyes caught his. He knew her first thought was to sit near him, but Mr. Polk seemed to think otherwise and pointed to the back of the room. He made her sit in the back by Neisha and Bryanna.

Marcus wanted to look back, but he didn't want Neisha to think he was trying to stare at her or something. So Marcus decided the best way to get Neisha's attention was to play it cool. Be the player he was, by letting her see she couldn't get all the boys to try to impress her.

Lynda walked by him and told the teacher, "Detention my behind," and he couldn't help but say something to this sexy girl right in front of him. He knew she wanted him; he liked her too, but he wanted a challenge, and Neisha was definitely that challenge.

Lynda kept her ground when making up a good comeback to Marcus's "beautiful behind" comment, and he had to admire that because most girls would trip over it, but she seemed to like the attention she was getting from him. Marcus knew that if he wanted to get some of that, he could, any day and any time. He

13

didn't know why he kept thinking about Neisha, when he could obviously get with half if not all the girls at Wilson High.

While Lynda was walking through the aisle to the back of the room, after flirting with Marcus, he couldn't help but stare at her from behind. He knew that she knew that he was checking her out, and that turned him on even more about Lynda because she was confident enough to make sure Marcus knew that he could have a taste of that whenever he was ready.

As his eyes lingered on Lynda as he followed her all the way up to her seat, they moved up to the direction of Neisha, who was sitting right next to her. Marcus being the attractive person that he was, didn't find it unusual to see girls staring at him during class, but it was the fact that the girl who was staring at him, oh so hard, was Neisha Thompson.

He couldn't believe it, but once he noticed her still checking him out, he knew for sure that Neisha wanted him. Automatically, Marcus's player attitude came out and it got the best of him. He tapped his boy Drew on the shoulder and told him what went down with the whole "Neisha-Marcus eye tag" confrontation.

Drew did not believe this. How and why in the world would a girl like Neisha be dumb enough to want to get at a big time Clique Boy like Marcus? "How in the world am I supposed to believe that Neisha Thompson was staring at you?"

"Why wouldn't she? Look, I bet she's still looking at me. Shawty was looking mesmerized when I was back there checkin' her out," Marcus said in a low whisper. "Look back there and see for yourself."

 # THE BOY IS MINE!

Drew turned in his seat to see if what Marcus was saying was true. Sure enough, Little Miss Stuck Up was staring, *hard*.

"Damn, boy, I don't know what you do, but you do it well," Drew told Marcus while giving him a play.

"I told you," Marcus said, grinning from ear to ear, "Once I want something, most likely I'm gonna get it."

"Yeah, but what makes you think she's gonna *give* it?" Drew asked Marcus, snickering. "Just 'cause she has a staring problem, doesn't mean she's gonna be crazy enough to give it up to you."

Marcus winked and said, "Every chick gives it up to me."

They exchanged another play, and Drew shook his head. "I still can't believe ol' girl is interested in you." He turned to Louis, who was being left out of the whole conversation. "Louis, why is this boy tryna get play from Neisha?"

"*Neisha?*" Louis said taken aback. "When did all this happen?"

Annoyed, Marcus answered, "When your dumb butt was listening to what Mr. P was sayin'."

Louis brushed that comment off. "Well, what happened?" Since Drew was closer to Louis, he told him exactly what happened in the last six minutes, action by action.

"Wow, boy, you got serious game," Louis said to Marcus, giving him his props for staying cool during the situation, no matter how awkward it might have been. "So what are you gonna do to keep her in play? You gotta let her know you're interested."

"Yeah, I know," Marcus said. He sighed, uninterestedly scoping the classroom. "But me being the person I am, that

15

shouldn't be too hard to accomplish." He looked down at his pants. "Once she gets some of this, she'll stay wanting more." Marcus and Drew joined in on another fist bump, Louis, on the other hand, seemed agitated by Marcus's lack of seriousness. "Stop being stupid, for real," he said to both Marcus and Drew.

Drew and Marcus finally calmed down from their perverted joke. "All right then, I guess I'll try to give her some of my famous 'Marcus Hamilton Charm'," Marcus said.

Drew shared a look of disbelief with Louis. "This man's stupid. This is *Neisha Thompson* we're talking about; if you tryna get into *her* pants you need more than your charm," Drew told Louis.

"A condom?" Marcus answered.

Drew and Louis rolled their eyes in exasperation. Marcus quickly changed his mind, "I don't know, I'll write her a note or something." It was the only *sweet* thing he could think of that he believed would somehow get the girl of his dreams attention.

Louis gave them a look of disbelief. "A *note?*" he asked.

"Yeah, a note," Marcus answered. "What else can I do, seeing as how we're in the middle of class? It's not like I can turn around and scream her name out in front of everybody."

Louis didn't care what he said. He knew if it were Marcus, he would've had her number by now. "That's the dumbest thing I have ever heard," he said.

"Nah, let's see where he's going with this." Drew said. He thought the idea was stupid too, but he wanted Marcus to see for himself that Neisha wasn't the type of girl who falls for a dumb high school letter, no matter who wrote it. "I wanna see what he has to say."

Marcus's palms began to sweat and he moved around uncomfortably in his chair because he was beginning to get a sick feeling in his stomach. What was he supposed to say to this girl? *Hey, I've wanted to hook up with you since I first saw you.* No way was he going to say that, especially with his boys sitting only inches away from him. They were expecting him to write something smooth, but the truth is, Marcus could hardly *ever* successfully stay cool, calm, and collected around Neisha.

He shook his head. "Oh no, I don't wanna write it. How 'bout one of y'all write it for me?" he asked.

"Not me," Louis automatically said. No way was his friend's fate going to lie in his hands because of his bad writing skills.

Drew sighed. "Ugh, somebody give me a pen." Louis wanted to be helpful, seeing as how he wasn't doing anything else, and gave Drew his pen. Drew had no clue what he was going to write to Neisha. "What do you want me to say?" he asked Marcus.

"Whatever you think is gonna let me get some of that faster," Marcus replied. Yeah, he knew that was a jackass answer, but he knew that if he was to say, "Tell her that I think she's cute and that I like her," his boys would clown him until he graduated.

But Marcus knew that deep inside, he would pay the price of their jokes, if he could only man up.

Marcus kept looking over at Drew to see what he was writing. Drew's hand moved really fast against the paper, and he wore this weird grin. Marcus knew his boy well enough to

17

know that whenever Drew grinned like that, he was doing something he had no business doing.

Drew, on the other hand, had a good time trying to write something he thought Marcus would say. He didn't know whether or not he should put that he thought she was one of the finest girls at school, or if he could have her number. All he knew was that he was really happy to not be Marcus—the guy Neisha would think wrote the note. If Marcus saw what Drew wrote, he would definitely freak out, so he tried to cover the paper up with his hand. Louis and Marcus were peering over his shoulder, trying to get a good look. Drew knew that Marcus was good at getting the ladies, but he also knew that if Marcus got Neisha, it would be all because of him. All he knew was that Marcus better give him his props if Neisha did give him some.

It was a little funny to him, trying to put the swag Marcus has with the ladies on a sheet of paper; he couldn't help but laugh. Just thinking how Neisha would react to the note put a grin on his face. Girls are so funny acting when it comes to guys writing those letters. Drew thought that when boys do that for girls, it's kind of like the boy is whipped. But Marcus wasn't the type of guy to let a girl get under his skin like that … hopefully.

Damn. Marcus thought to himself. *Why in the world did I let Drew, of all people, write this note? He"s probably telling her how fine she is and asking her for her phone number. I like the girl and all, but I wanna ask her for her number myself.* Marcus then thought about something: *Why am I even trippin" over this? I'm a Clique Boy; I don"t get sprung off a girl, no matter what. I'mma just treat her like I treat everyone else. Man, I*

18

don"t know why I'm even trying so hard for this stuck-up girl anyway; Lynda will let me hit real easily, so why do I need Neisha to help prove myself to Drew and Torean? I'll just get the note from Drew before he passes it to her, and I can get over this whole day.

But too late, Drew just turned around, and told the guy behind him, Sam, to give the note to Neisha. Marcus tried to stop Drew before he gave it to Sam, but Drew, rushed the boy to passes it to her. Marcus knew he was doing this on purpose; now it was too late to retrieve the note. Talk about being pissed off.

Marcus pushed Drew on the shoulder. "Damn, didn't you just see me tryna get the note from you?" he said, almost in a whining voice. "I mean, I didn't even get to see what you wrote. That's messed up what you just did, man."

"Man, get over it. She has the note, and by now, she's probably writing back. When ol' boy passes it back to me, you can write back so that *you* can see what I wrote, a'ight? I mean, Damn, if you wanted to see what was written, you shoulda wrote the note yourself. Over here tryna push on somebody. You need to calm your behind down," Drew said, looking opposite Marcus, as if what Marcus said really did get under his skin.

NEISHA

Wednesday, 11:00 A.M.
STUDY HALL

As Neisha unfolded the note, a rush of anticipation came over her. She placed the note back down, figuring that whatever the note said, could wait until class was over. That was only in what? Ten minutes? She could wait.

But why should I? Neisha thought. *If he took the time to write this note, maybe I should stop being stupid and just read it. What"s the worse he could say? „Neisha, you need to stop starin"at me because I don"tlike you"." That is so unlikely. Just take a chance and grow up. Getting turned down by a super sexy boy isn"t he worst thing that can happen. I think.*

Neisha picked the note back up from her desk. She could tell Bryanna was watching her from the corner of her eye, but Neisha didn't care; Bre had a chance to read this note, now it was her turn.

Her eyes were moving all across the paper. She wasn't able to concentrate on only one part of the paragraph, so she closed her eyes and reopened them, focusing on one word at a time. Trying not to skip ahead, she read the note she thought Marcus wrote:

Neisha,

I saw you staring at me a few minutes ago and I wanna know why. I know I look good & all, but I've never seen any 1 check me out the way that you did. I think it's kind of sexy that u aren't afraid to look at something I know U want. I mean, if u wanna get at me, all u have 2 do is ask because I'm DEFINITELY feeling you right now. If u wanna talk, u know where to find me. But if Ur 2 nervous to come by my crew, u should call me. My # is 555-3615.

P.S. If you're not scared, u can give me yours 2.

When Neisha was done reading the note, she felt numb. She couldn't believe Marcus had the nerve to be cocky, even in a letter. Neisha looked at Bryanna; Bryanna returned her gaze. "I told you it was crazy," she said moving her head in the direction of Marcus and his boys. "He is seriously trippin', girl. I don't know if that's his way of trying to be flirtatious, but what he wrote was really conceited."

Neisha glanced at Marcus, and then back at her friend. "He has a Damn good reason to be," she said, showing a mouth full of teeth.

21

Bryanna didn't find that funny. "So you're gonna let him passes with that? You must *really* like him then. If that was me, I would've ripped that note right up 'cause no guy's gonna front on me like that," she told her friend. Bryanna knew that when Neisha liked someone, she wasn't going to put them on fault for anything; they're always perfect in her eyes.

"Well, he's not fronting on me, is he? I can reply saying anything I want, and I will. And for the record, I do not like him, so shut up," Neisha said in whisper. "I won't tell him anything he doesn't need to hear."

"Whatever," Bryanna mumbled, as she once again focused back on the teacher, who for some reason was still talking.

Neisha maneuvered the paper on her desk so she could write on it. Out the corner of her eye, she could see that Lynda was being nosy, trying to see who wrote her the letter, so she repositioned the paper. Neisha grabbed her pen and began to write her reply, knowing this was just what Marcus needed to get him right back down to earth.

Marcus stared at the clock, wondering why this class was taking so long to be over. He really wanted to leave before Neisha replied to the letter. Marcus didn't want her to write back something mean or anything, so he figured the only way he wouldn't be rejected is if he just didn't wait for her reply. Only four minutes were left in class, so he didn't have too long to wait.

Although he fronted like he didn't want the note, he wondered what was taking her so long to write back.

Drew held something up in his face. Quickly, he retrieved it before anyone could see that a boy like him was passing notes in class. He opened the note and moved it under his desk so that nobody knew what he was doing. Then, he started to read:

Marcus,

What R U talking about? I wasn't looking at you or whatever you're saying. If you thought I was looking at you, you got it ALL wrong.

Well, a reply 2 what you said about me being sexy or whatever, thanks...I guess.

And NO you can't have my # . . . yet, but keep working at it and you can.

P.S. Next time hand me the note yourself. ♥♥

When Marcus was done reading the reply, he wore a wide smile. Drew and Louis hunched their shoulders as if to ask, "What went down?" Marcus handed them the note.

Drew was the first one to read the note, and then he handed it over to Louis, who took the note and scanned the paper. Each of their faces showed a distinct sign of laughter by the time they were done reading the letter. Louis looked at Marcus and snorted. "P.S. next time hand me the note yourself? Yeah, she's definitely feeling you," he said.

"I know, I know," Marcus said, smiling. "When I want something, I get it. And I'm *definitely* gonna get her."

Louis moved closer to Marcus. He looked at the clock and then back at his boy. "You just gotta get at her before the bell rings," Louis said. Drew nodded his head in agreement.

"I will, I will, don't worry about me. As you can see, I have two bad chicks going after me right now, so I think I can handle it," Marcus bragged.

Drew looked at him questioningly; his brows raised high on his face, and asked, "What other girl is tryna get at you?"

Marcus answered, "Lynda."

"Oh, so you're still gonna get at that, then?" Louis asked, although he already knew the answer.

"Yeah, what's a player supposed to do when two beautiful women are around and oh so tempting?"

Louis answered, "Try to see which one will give it up faster?"

Marcus didn't have time to answer Louis's question because at that same time the bell had rung, signaling the end of Study Hall.

WAHIDA CLARK PRESENTS

UNDER PRESSURE

Y.A.
YOUNG ADULT

A YOUNG ADULT NOVEL BY

RASHAWN HUGHES

ONE

As Quentin, Torry, and Chase rode in QB's truck toward Shea Stadium, they could barely contain their excitement as they bounced and sang along with the hook on Neyo and Fab's single *"You Make Me Better."*

Torry and Chase had never been to a professional baseball game. They were clowning around like children instead of the grown men they claimed to be. QB was just as excited because he was able to give them an opportunity to experience something other than hanging out on the block. Today was a special day; they were celebrating the hard work and sacrifice Chase and Torry put into achieving their General Equivalency Diploma (G.E.D).

Once they entered the home of the New York Mets, both Chase and Torry looked around Shea Stadium in amazement. This was the Mets final year of playing in this stadium. The organization had finally invested in a 21st century stadium with all the amenities to make it more fan-friendly and more importantly, profitable.

This place is huge, Chase thought. The smell of roasted peanuts, hot dogs, and buttered popcorn wafted in the air.

Families were busy trying to find their seats. Happy faces, exciting sounds of children, and laughter generated throughout the stadium. Children ran around like they were hooked on caffeine.

Torry tapped Chase on the arm. "Yo, peep shorty right there in the Apple Bottoms."

"Yeah, I'm on her," Chase replied. After a quick glance he thought, *My family never did things like this.*

UNDER PRESSURE

QB yelled out to them, "C'mon, I want to get y'all something." He led them to the concession stand to purchase some memorabilia. Both Chase and Torry wanted a Mets 'fitted,' which QB learned was slang for a baseball cap. QB was thinking more along the lines of an autographed photo or maybe an autographed bat.

Both Chase and Torry had enough hats, but this was their day so he purchased the fitted's for them. Torry picked out an oversized black and blue Mets fitted, with the orange N.Y. symbol stenciled on the front. Because of the color blue, Chase changed his mind and selected a black Chicago White Sox fitted. It matched his brand new Gino Green pullover that he'd just copped a few days ago. Gino Green Global was the hottest clothing line to hit the set since Sean John.

QB purchased both hats for the boys even though he knew Chase selected the black Sox cap because it matched his gang colors. QB didn't want to ruin the day with an argument about that so he held back what he wanted to say. Instead he led them both to find their seats.

As usual the boys walked with a hip-hop swagger, which caused a few people to stare at them. Whether they were admiring their style or reinforcing their own stereotypes, it amazed QB how young black men were perceived. QB knew from experience that because of their unique way of doing things they were looked at with suspicious eyes. *Misunderstood should be the epitaph tattooed on the faces of Black and Latin youth*, QB thought.

They sat three rows behind the Mets dugout along the first base line. They could hear the players in the dugout talking, laughing, and getting ready for the game. QB looked around noticing how well the grounds people kept the field. Even the dirt was manicured. *I have to get these groundskeepers to do my lawn*, he thought.

Ten minutes after they sat down, Chase pulled out his BlackBerry and dialed his man.

"Yo, speak."

"What up, B? This Chase."

What's good, my dude, where you at?"

"We're laid up in Shea Stadium right now checking out the Mets."

"Yeah right," replied B.

"Turn on your television, kid."

"What channel?"

"I don't know, try UPN or that ESPN station," Chase answered.

"Hold up, let me find it." There was a pause as B channel surfed. "I got it. The Mets, right?"

Chase looked for the television cameras. "Can you see us?" he asked.

"Nah, they got two cats on the screen talking about the game. Where y'all niggas sitting?

"Right behind the Mets dugout. I got that black fitted on. Plus it looks like we're the only niggas in the building. It shouldn't be hard to spot us."

"I'll check for you when the game starts," B said. There was an unusual pause. B was contemplating whether or not he should tell Chase what was being said about him since Chase was his boy. "Check it, my dude, I don't know how to tell you this but Showtyme told niggas' last night to wash you up. Something about you pressing him about wanting out of the Henchmen," he said.

"Who me?"

"Yeah nigga, you."

"When he tell y'all that?"

"I just told you ... last night."

Perspiration began forming on his bald head. Chase sat there in disbelief. There was another pause. During that awkward moment Chase felt his safety net of being in one of the most notorious gangs in New York begin to unravel.

"You there, Chase?"

"Yeah man, I'm here. Let me ask you something, B. Where do you stand?"

UNDER PRESSURE

"What kind of question is that? Where the hell do you think I stand? I wouldn't be telling you jack if I was gonna get at you."

"I hear you."

"My dude, on some bull, make sure you keep my name out of this. I don't want to get caught up in this drama. You should lay low for a minute so I can try to work things out."

"C'mon B, you know how I get down."

"No doubt. Yo, you hear me though. Someone is banging down my door right now. It's probably this hoodrat chick that wants me to crush it. Hit me up when you get back around the way."

"A'ight, B, I'll holla," Chase said, ending the call. He didn't know what to make of the news, but he knew craziness lay before him. He sighed, thinking how being in the Henchmen was madness, but getting out was as dangerous as a landmine.

After B hung up the phone, he took a couple of pulls on the hydro he was puffing, and when he became nice and paranoid he called Showtyme. Unfortunately, it wasn't to try to straighten things out.

After hitting the end button on his phone, Chase sunk in his seat and buried his head in his hands as if he had a headache.

Torry, too busy checking out how the players walked, stretched, and prepared for the game, didn't notice Chase's change of attitude. Torry sat there with his mouth and eyes wide open as if Beyonce and Alicia Keys were mud wrestling on the pitcher's mound.

"Look, there's Willie Randolph," Torry said, pointing to the Mets manager who was struggling to hold on to his job. He was talking with a few fans behind home plate.

QB smiled. *I hope he weathers this storm, for it's good to have a black manager representing in the Big Apple.*

Torry turned to him. "I know what you're thinking, QB."

"What's that, little bruh?"

"I know you're feeling the Mets having a black manager."

QB smiled. "Who the hell do you think you are, Cleo?" QB was amazed at how his students thought they knew him. The truth of the matter is some actually did, which was a good thing. Hopefully, some of his ways would rub off on them. "You got that, and you know what?"

"What?"

"It's long overdue. They should have been hired a black—"

Cutting him off, Chase turned toward QB with his mouth twisted up. "C'mon QB—not now with that black mess."

QB looked at him like he was crazy. "What you say?"

"I don't want to hear that right now, QB."

With a raised brow QB looked at him and tightened his grip on his chair. He took a few deep breaths, a tactic he learned from his wife to prevent saying something he would later regret. He noticed that something was bothering Chase since he made that call. QB possessed the ability to read the attitude and body language of his students like a closed captioning for the hearing impaired. However, that was no excuse for Chase to come at him like that and more importantly it was no excuse for him to undermine the importance of hiring a black man in a profession that was historically biased. He exhaled and wondered to himself, *When will these kids get it?*

Torry looked at Chase and shook his head. He attempted to change the subject. "QB, you really came through with these tickets. That's what's up and I just want to thank you. It's definitely a good look," he said.

QB turned to him then glanced at Chase. "It's nothing. I promised you guys that I would do this if you passed your G.E.D. and you guys stepped up and did it ... Now that's a good look. When you put in work, as you both like to say, your efforts will be rewarded." QB's cell phone rang. He looked at the caller-ID and decided not to take the call. Looking out toward center field, he continued, "That's what this is all about—putting in that work because the only place success comes before work is in the dictionary," he said.

Torry thought about that for a minute, then reached out to give QB a pound. "Ain't that right, Chase?"

Chase, lost in his own thoughts stared out into the clear sky, thinking about what he needed to do in order to get up out of the Henchmen.

QB noticed the worried look on his face. "Chase, what's up with you? Is everything all right?" he asked.

In an attempt to hide his concerns, Chase looked down avoiding QB's stare. "Yeah, QB, it's all good."

QB knew he was lying, so he continued to probe. "You sure?"

Chase looked up and put on as much of a smile as his face could muster. He knew he was wrong for coming at QB like that. "I'm good, QB. I just have a few things that I have to handle. I didn't mean to come at you like that; you know you're my nig ..." Chase tried to stop at the last second but it was too late.

QB threw his hand up like he was stopping traffic. "How many times do I have to tell you that I'm not your N-word? You act like you purchased me at an auction or something, because that's where N-words were sold." QB looked at him with disapproval, and then continued, "Chase, do you know where that word comes from?"

"Yeah, QB, I know. It comes from the Latin word Niger, which is actually a country in West Africa. For West Africans the word simply meant the color black, but somewhere around the 1800's it became a symbol of white racism.

"If that's the case, why do you keep using it?" Chase didn't respond. "You need to understand that that word was imposed on African American people by whites because they wanted to make us feel inferior; less than them so they could justify using us for our labor. White people, during that time, knew that in order to make people of color feel subservient they had to not only make us feel different, but make us see ourselves as less than worthy. The N-word, whether it's spelled with an 'er' or an 'a', is the term they used and here you are in 2010 using it like it's some kind of term of endearment." QB shook his head in disgust. "It's crazy."

Neither of the boys said anything. This was one of those arguments where they both knew they had no wins.

QB looked at them both. "Do you two know how important a name or title is? Don't you two understand how easy it is for you to hurt or kill somebody you call the N-word? Don't you see the connection? The N-word is akin to worthlessness, and this makes it much easier for you to get at someone who you consider a N-word."

Torry glanced at Chase. "Why did you get him started?" he whispered.

"You damn right he got me started. Think about it. It is much more difficult for you to hurt someone you call your brother. Listen to how it sounds. 'Let's ride on those N-words,' or 'Let's kill that N-word is much easier to say or do as opposed to Let's kill that brother.'" QB paused to let his words sink in. "It's a big difference—right?" Neither of the boys replied. "You guys better know that how you see yourself will determine just how far you both make it in this world."

"You got that, QB," Chase said.

"Yeah, I know I got that, the problem is you getting it." QB looked him directly in his eyes. "I'm going to give you a pass this time, but don't get it twisted, I can still break one of you young dudes down like a shotgun." QB playfully shot a quick, hard jab into the air startling the middle aged white man sitting in front of him. QB apologized. They all had a good laugh. "Chase, seriously though, if you need to talk or need me for anything know that I am here for you, all right?" QB added.

"I know, QB," Chase said, feeling guilty.

"Let's get something to eat," QB said, wanting to break the tension.

"Can we get some beer, QB?" asked Chase.

QB looked at him. "Yeah, something is definitely wrong with you. You know that's not happening. Your grandmother would kill both of us if she knew I was out here letting you drink."

Chase sucked his teeth as he looked for the vendor. "C'mon, QB, she's not going to find out."

Even though QB wouldn't mind a cold beer himself, he knew doing the right thing was a full-time job, especially when dealing with the youth. They were always looking and watching even when you thought they weren't. "You heard what I said?" Now, if you want some popcorn and sodas you better call that vendor over here before she heads the other way."

"Damn, shorty is hot," Torry said, eyeing the vendor.

"Where?" asked Chase.

"Over there," he said, nodding his head toward the beautiful young lady who stood about five and half feet tall. She had her hair pulled back in a ponytail accentuating her pretty brown, oval shaped eyes. *She's a natural beauty*, thought Torry.

Chase was hypnotized. *She has to be mixed with something, maybe some Indian or something. Nothing should be that good-looking*, he thought. She was a caramel complexion, with a body, and a smile that read 'enter here and find your way to heaven.' "That's definitely wifey material," Chase said.

Chase and Torry watched her make her way down the aisles of the stadium. QB watched the boys as they looked open like a twenty-four hour deli. He tried to remember if he acted like that over women when he was their age.

"Popcorn, peanuts, soda and cracker jacks. Get your popcorn, peanuts, soda and cracker jacks," yelled the young lady in a voice that melted Chase's troubles away.

"Excuse me, miss, over here," Chase yelled, standing and waving his hand creating way too much attention.

She stopped twice before making her way over to them. "What would you like, sir?" she asked, showing off a smile that cut through all of Chase's player instincts.

Chase returned her smile. "What's up, ma? I'll take some popcorn and directions."

"Excuse me?"

"I would like some popcorn and directions."

She blushed. "Directions where?" she asked.

"To your heart," Chase said, licking his lips like he was LL Cool J.

QB and Torry simultaneously burst out laughing.

The smile on the young lady's face told Chase that he had a shot. "I doubt you could find my heart if I led you there by your hand."

Looking into her eyes, Chase extended his hand. "Try me. My name is Chase." He peered down at QB and Torry. "Ignore these guys; they don't know how to act in the presence of someone as beautiful as you. And you are?"

She twisted her glossed lips, giving him a well-deserved smirk. "If you were really looking to get to my heart," she said, pointing to her name tag pinned directly above her heart, "You would know my name is Lexi."

"Aaahhhh, she got you there, playa," said Torry.

Chase shot daggers at Torry. "Why are you hatin' on the kid?"

"Look! I work on commission so I don't have time to waste."

Chase cleared his throat. "Trust me, you're not wasting your time, shorty."

"Excuse me—first of all, my name is not Shorty, it's Lexi," she said, rolling her eyes.

"My bad, Lexi," he said with a smile.

Silence settled between them two. QB decided to intervene. "Pardon my little brother. He refers to all women as shortie."

The young lady smiled at QB. "It's okay." She then looked at Chase. "Maybe one day he'll learn that there is a difference between the two."

QB smiled, and then nodded at Chase. He ordered three popcorns, some peanuts, and three large sodas. "That'll be fourteen dollars," Lexi said.

UNDER PRESSURE

Chase reached into his pocket stunting like he was going to pay for it. As the young lady spoke with her next customer, QB gave Chase a 'stop fronting' look. QB momentarily thought about letting him pay for it, but he didn't want to embarrass him in case he didn't have the money. He winked at Chase. "I got it, Chase, you paid for breakfast." He then handed the young lady a twenty. "Here you go."

After QB got his change, Chase extended his hand. "It was nice meeting you." With his number palmed he shook Lexi's hand. "Make sure you call me with those directions. I'll forever be lost without them."

Lexi smirked at his corny line. "I'll think about it." She put the piece of paper in her pocket and smiled then headed up the rows of fans, with what seemed like an extra bounce in her step.

After she was out of earshot, Torry placed his head on Chase's shoulder. "I'll take some popcorn and directions to your heart." In between laughs, he added, "That was the lamest line I've ever heard."

"Not to mention the most embarrassing one," QB added.

They were cracking up. Even Chase couldn't help but laugh, but he immediately started singing Maino's new single "Hi Haters'." People around them started laughing not really knowing what they were laughing about, proving that laughter is contagious.

Regaining his composure QB interrupted them. "A'ight you two, chill-out. That's enough. They're about to sing the *National Anthem.* Take those hats off and stand up."

"What? C'mon, QB why we gotta stand up?" Chase questioned. "This country has no allegiance to us nig—I mean, brothers. So why should we pledge our allegiance to it?"

QB was shocked by his response, but seized the moment. "That may very well be true, but right now I'm asking you to stand out of respect."

Chase put his soda down, knowing QB meant business. They both took off their hats and stood up. QB whispered, "Chase, do me a favor … be easy with that black stuff." They all smiled.

W·CLARK
PUBLISHING
60 Evergreen Place, Suite 904
East Orange New Jersey 07018

ATTENTION:

We are seeking submissions for the
Wahida Clark Presents Young Adult Line.

Submission Guidelines:

✓ No emailed submissions accepted.

✓ Submissions must be typed and double spaced.

✓ No handwritten submissions.

www.wcpyoungadult.com

WAHIDA CLARK PRESENTS

NINETY NINE
PROBLEMS

A Young Adult Novel BY

GLORIA DOTSON-LEWIS

WITHDRAWN

CPSIA information can be obtained
at www.ICGtesting.com
Printed in the USA
LVHW02s2151010818
585623LV00018B/230/P